Murder in Hell

A Brick North Mystery

by Augustine Meijer

Copyright © 2021 Augustine Meijer

All rights reserved

This novel's story and characters are fictitious. Certain long-standing institutions, agencies, and public offices are mentioned, but the characters involved are wholly imaginary. No part of this book may be reproduced, stored in a retrieval system, or transmitted in any form or by any means, electronic, mechanical, photocopying, recording, or otherwise, without express written permission of the publisher.

ISBN-13: 978-1-7352291-5-7 (Paperback Edition)

Cover design by Mark Bussemeier
Photo used by under license © Jhandersen, Dreamstime.com

Also by Augustine Meijer

Murder at Lakeland
Murder Unholy

A note from the author:

I grew up in the Twin Cities of Benton Harbor and Saint Joseph, Michigan. In this book, I've taken the license of combining these two cities into the fictional town of LaSalle Harbor. If you're familiar with Berrien County, Michigan (renamed Douglas County in this series), or the Twin Cities, you'll note some place and road names are familiar. While I've changed some business names, other long-closed businesses are called by their name, including "Aristo Cleaners," which my maternal grandparents, Charles and Iota Kizer, owned and operated.

I'm proud of the community I grew up in, and while the adage that you can never go home again is true, one can certainly do so in their memory.

This book is dedicated to the men and women of law enforcement. In small villages and giant metropolises, those who wear a badge put aside their problems, step beyond their limitations, and find a way to make our communities better places to live. A sincere thank you to those with whom I work and have become defacto beta-readers. Finally, with love to my wife, who has put up with me writing into the wee hours as I struggle to get thoughts onto paper.

Murder in Hell

Chapter 1

Brick North's first few weeks in Hell were a blur. He had arrived in the fifty-four Dodge pickup he bought at auction from the Michigan Department of Natural Resources. After unloading his few belongings and supplies, he began working on the cottage his parents had left him. Truth-be-told, as an only child, his parents had left him everything.

Hell, Michigan, was barely a wide spot in the road in southern Livingston County. While only seventeen miles from Ann Arbor and the University of Michigan and sixty miles from Detroit, the contrast was so great that Hell might as well have been in the primeval forests of Europe. Lush with both conifers and deciduous trees, and with gently rolling hills, it was easy to see why the original German settlers had stopped and stayed.

The first order of business had been to begin the massive chore of dusting, sweeping, mopping, and cleaning. North had no idea when his father had last used the cottage. His mother had died while he was fighting Nazis in France back in forty-four. His father died five years ago in fifty-two, and the tiny house hadn't been used since then. The most recent magazine in the living room was a July forty-seven copy of "Life." North speculated that it could well have been a decade since anyone had visited the cottage. If the overgrowth around the property was any indication, it was a long time since anyone had been there.

North was pleasantly surprised that the two-bedroom cottage now featured only a single bedroom, his youthful room having been turned into a bathroom. It was not important when the house had been remodeled; all that mattered was there was no more outhouse. With winter approaching, Brick was agreeable with whoever's decision it was to plumb the house. All he had to do was get the water out of the well and into the plumbing.

The evening of the ninth day in Hell, he finally got the pump working, its filter having been filled with silt. With running water, a full bath, a comfortable bedroom, and a living room – kitchen combination, the cottage, though small, was considerably larger and better appointed than his room had been back at the Swanson Hotel in LaSalle Harbor. He lit a fire in the woodstove, dumped a can of beans into a pan, and placed it on the stove to heat. A glass of Old Quaker bourbon sat on the table along with the Colt .38 he'd purchased.

He switched on the old Crosley radio on the kitchen counter, tuned it into WLQV out of Detroit, and waited for the tubes to warm up to catch the final game of the World Series. To everyone's surprise, the Milwaukee Braves had tied the Yankees, leading to a seventh game.

While North ate the beans out of the old enamelware pot with a spoon and sipped at the bourbon, he contemplated the events that had led him here. He ran his fingers through his thick wavy hair as he recalled the young rapist who had fallen down the terrazzo steps of the Safety Building while being taken to a holding cell. How the Grand Jury had recommended that he be indicted for deliberately harming that rapist who was the son of an up-and-coming politician, and how he had been placed on leave awaiting his trial.

Augustine Meijer "Murder in Hell"

North was a realist. He understood that things often blow up, and there is nothing one can do but to continue to pull oneself up. He was reminded of what a philosophy professor turned soldier had told him during the war, "As Confucius said, 'We are all like water seeking the easiest path downhill.'" Life is either slipping downhill or deciding to pull oneself up. North chose the latter.

Meanwhile, fifteen miles to the east of where he sat, someone closed their fingers around the windpipe of a University of Michigan coed. The rough hands increased their pressure until they felt the crunching of cartilage, and the coed stopped struggling. The newly created murderer felt both a rush of nausea as well as a strange euphoria as he looked at the body of the brunette that lay beneath him. He climbed off her still form, pulled on his clothes, and used a sheet to wrap her body.

North washed his cookware and looked out the kitchen window as the first snowflakes of the season drifted to the ground. Many of those flakes would still be in shaded areas, compressed under more layers of snow when spring came. He went outside and brought in more firewood, noting that he would need a lot more wood should he end up spending the winter in Hell.

He listened to the World Series game, bottom of the eighth, and Milwaukee was ahead five to nothing. Much to his consternation, the Braves won the game in New York, taking the series. He turned off the radio and sat in the dark, sipping bourbon until he eventually fell asleep.

He was awakened by a vehicle driving slowly past the house. He rolled out of the chair and sought cover behind the old sofa. His mind had flashed back and showed him a convoy of Nazi vehicles and infantry. North searched but could not find his carbine. He lay in the cold mud along the side of the road as platoon after platoon of German soldiers marched by. Weaponless and away from his unit, his heart pounded inside his chest. As the last platoon marched past, he heard one of the soldiers cry out, "*Leutnant, da ist etwas im Gebüsch.*" "There's something in the bushes." North cringed as multiple Mauser M712 submachines guns cut through the foliage on the opposite side of the road. Confident they had destroyed their target, the Germans moved on.

North lay sweating on the hooked rug in the living room. He was still there when the morning light streamed through the window. His Bulova showed that it was a quarter of seven. Shaking off the fog, he pushed his lean frame off the floor and into the bathroom before getting the stove hot enough to perc a pot of coffee.

After downing the coffee and a bowl of Wheaties, North pulled on a pair of boots and slipped into the old red and black plaid Mackinaw his dad had left in the closet. He took a walk carrying the bean can from the previous night's supper. The early snow was already melting in the sun when he found a fence post well away from any buildings. He put the can on the post, walked about twenty-five feet away, and removed the new Colt Detective Special from its holster under his right arm. He flipped the cylinder open and spun it, making sure all six rounds were there before snapping it back into the frame. The knurled trigger felt familiar under his finger as he pulled it. The can jumped from the post and into a pile of brush about twelve feet back from the dirt road.

As North bent to retrieve the can, he saw off-white fabric under the brush. He gingerly lifted one of several pine boughs that had been carefully laid over the material; a human foot protruded from what appeared to be a bedsheet. Looking around, he could see in the muddy ground where the body had been dragged from the edge of the road. North lowered the bough and gave a cursory look at the scene. Fresh tire tracks were evident. From the width of the tracks and their distance from one another, they appeared to be from a small truck and not a car.

He quickly walked back to his cottage, trying to burn the images into his head. If the weather warmed or there were additional rain or snow, the drag marks and tire tracks could disappear. He retrieved the keys to the truck at the cottage and drove the mile and a half into Hell. "If I end up here for long, I'm going to need to get a phone," he thought aloud. "Then again, I wonder if there's even a phone line out here they can connect to?"

In town, he found a payphone outside the small general store. He picked up the receiver and dialed "0." A moment later, a well-trained female voice answered, "Operator."

"I need the Sheriff's office," North spoke in a clear voice.

"One moment, while I connect your call." There were a series of clicks before the phone was answered by a gruff-sounding female, "Livingston County Sheriff's Department."

"My name is Richard North; I just found a body near my cottage on Hickman Court off of Weiman Road on the south side of Hi-Land Lake."

There was a pause before the Sheriff's office responded, "You say you found a body?"

"Yes. I didn't want to disturb the scene, but it appears to be a Caucasian female."

"How is it you happened to find the body?"

"Tell you what, send someone out, and we can play show-and-tell. My cottage has a sign out front, reads 'North's End,' I'll be there." Brick hung up the phone, stepped into the store to buy some cigarettes, and drove back to the cottage. It was nearly forty-five minutes before a brown and white Sheriff's vehicle pulled onto Hickman Court. An older deputy stepped out of the car and squared his brown wool, flat-rimmed trooper hat on his head. North stepped out to meet him.

"You Richard North?" the gravel-voiced deputy asked.

"I am," North took a pull on his cigarette. "People usually call me Rick."

"I'll be damned; you're Ricky North, Brian and Nora's boy? Heck, it has got to be twenty years since I've seen you," he stuck out his hand, "Dennis Deweiss."

North thought for a few moments before taking the offered hand, "Dennis, sure I remember you."

The deputy looked around through the bare trees, "I understand you found a body out here somewhere?"

"Yeah, I was plinking at a tin can down the lane when I came across it." North used his head to point down the road.

"Climb in," Deweiss offered, "let's go check it out."

North shook his head, "No, let's walk, so we don't drive over any evidence."

Deweiss gave him a quizzical look, "You sound like a cop."

"I'm on leave from the LaSalle Harbor PD."

North and Deputy Deweiss walked down the narrow dirt road, the moist soil compacting under their feet. In places, mud squirted up and over the top of their shoes with each step. He pointed as they walked, "The body is just past those trees." The scene was just as he'd left it. Twelve feet off the road, there was a pile of brush. North pointed out the tire tracks and drag marks, "Looks like someone stopped here and pulled the body out using the sheet as a litter."

Deweiss bent down and examined both the tire tracks and the drag marks, which he followed to a mound of pine branches and debris. North pointed to a dented pork and bean can, "That's the can that I was plinking at," he said, adding, "when I bent down to retrieve it, I saw that fabric poking out." The deputy moved just enough of the fauna covering the sheet to see the foot that North had seen an hour before.

"You have a phone I can use?"

Brick shook his head, "Nope, I had to drive into town to use one."

"Okay, you stay here and make certain no one disturbs this. I've got to call the Sheriff and the coroner. You good with that?"

A corner of North's mouth turned up in a smile, "It's just like being back at work, but without the pay." He pulled a cigarette out of the pocket of the Mackinaw and lit it, "Think you could grab a thermos of coffee on your way back?"

Deweiss laughed. "You want a doughnut with that?" he asked sarcastically.

The deputy's retort reminded him of conversations he'd had with his partner Barry Tiffin back in LaSalle Harbor, "Nah, I'm good."

Deweiss walked back to his car, leaving North alone with his thoughts. In under three weeks, he'd gone from a detective with a solid track record to indicted on felony charges and on leave without pay. While the felony charges were an issue, money was not. His parents had left him both the cottage and a large house in Grosse Pointe Shores. He had sold the house following his father's death. The proceeds of the sale, the equivalent of seven years' pay, had gone into the bank; this would be the first time he'd have to take advantage of those funds.

A formation of Canada Geese, probably the last of the season, kept North's attention, as did a stray marmalade-colored cat that kept just at the periphery of his vision. Pickings got scarce once the summer occupants of the cottages around Hi-Land Lake went home for the winter. "It's probably why our victim was placed here." North mused, "Normally, no one would be back here again for six months." He considered that thought for a moment, "So our murderer must have some connection to this area." He was on his fourth cigarette when Deweiss returned, followed by two other cars.

"North!" Deweiss called out as he approached, "Let me introduce you to Sheriff Drake, and that's our Coroner, Doctor Von Boren." The Sheriff, two decades younger than Deweiss, walked up with his hand extended, "Is it Richard, Rich, or Rick?" he asked as they shook hands.

"Most everyone calls me Brick," North responded.

"Call me Tom. Now tell me what you were doing out here and what you found."

"My cottage is down the lane. It's the one with the green Dodge pickup and the sign that reads 'North's End' out front. I wandered down here this morning around nine to get a feel for a new pistol I bought. Fired one shot, the tin can flew off to the left, followed it to that pile of brush, found what Deweiss has probably told you, and called your office. End of story."

Concern crossed Drake's face, "Where's the pistol now?"

"Secured in my cottage."

"Good, let's leave it there right now. If we find this person was shot, I'll want to take a look at that gun of yours."

"If I shot the victim, I sure wouldn't have come down here to do some target practice," North bristled.

"Unless you were trying to make us look the other way."

North thought about Drake's response. If the roles were reversed, he'd probably have the same answer.

"Now, stand back and let us do our jobs. Denny, make sure Mr. North keeps his distance." The Sheriff, deputy, and doctor walked over to the pile of brush. Deweiss and Drake pulled the branches off, uncovering an off-white bed sheet. Drake gave a nod in the direction of Von Boren, "Steve, let's see what we've got."

The coroner gently pulled at a corner of the sheet revealing the bare legs of what appeared to be a woman. He then walked to the other side, where he again gave the sheet another pull. The partially nude body of a young brunette was fully exposed to the midday light. Von Boren reminded North of Doc Howard back in LaSalle Harbor. He carefully lowered himself to one knee and began to call out his observations, "Female, fully developed, approximately twenty to twenty-five years old." He gently moved a leg, "Bruising to the external genitalia and inner thighs would suggest non-consensual coitus. There is also bruising along the torso and," he paused as he moved up her body, "yes, here it is, it would seem that she was strangled. I will speculate that her trachea was crushed. You can clearly see the antemortem bruising in a shape suggesting a pair of hands." The doctor held his hands out and imitated how she was strangled. "I'll know more after an autopsy, but that's what I've got so far."

Drake flicked the ashes off the cigarette he was smoking, "So, some bastard raped and strangled our victim. Any idea how long she's been dead?"

The doctor stood up and wiped his hands on his handkerchief, "Twelve to twenty-four hours; rigor has fully set in."

Drake looked at North, "Why don't we wander over to your cottage and have a chat." Brick nodded; five minutes later, they were walking in the front door. "Dennis tells me that he knew your folks," the Sheriff said as he lit a cigarette.

"And I vaguely remember him. He patrolled the area years ago and would stop and talk." North kept an eye on Drake; if the Sheriff noticed the empty bourbon bottle along with one yet-to-be-opened, he didn't mention it. "Are any of these other cottages occupied?"

North, who had just started putting a fresh pot of coffee together, shook his head, "I've been here almost three weeks; I spoke to one family as they were packing up for the winter; that was the first weekend I was here. Otherwise, it's been the squirrels and me."

"If Von Boren is right, our victim was dropped here last night. You notice any cars back here last night?"

North hoped the involuntary shiver at the thought of last night's nightmare wasn't noticeable, "I may have heard a car drive by, but I don't know what time it was."

"Drinking pretty heavily, were you?" the Sheriff's tone was nonaccusatory.

"Yankees lost the series, so I probably had a few."

The Sheriff nodded his understanding, "If I were smart, I would've put money on the Braves. No one expected them to win." Drake paused to crush out his cigarette, "So, tell me, who did you piss off to be put on leave?"

North gave the Sheriff an honest and complete answer to his question. "That's crap." the Sheriff blurted out. North bristled at Drake's response. "No, don't get me wrong, I believe you; I just hate politicians."

North checked the percolator, "Aren't sheriffs elected?"

Drake nodded his head, "I'm a lawman first and a politician second. I ran for Sheriff because the man I was working under was a politician first and used the office as a springboard for better things. He didn't give a shit about the office or the men who worked under him."

There was a knock on the door; North walked over and opened the door for Deputy Deweiss, "Sheriff, thought you'd want to know that I made a plaster cast of a tire track that has a distinctive cut across the tread."

"Good work, Dennis. Keep me updated on how the investigation is going."

The older deputy nodded, "Yes, sir."

North looked up from the cup of coffee he was pouring, "You know, I can help you with this investigation. I've got some pretty decent detective skills."

Drake took the offered cup, "You're currently not a sworn officer."

Grinning, North answered, "No, but I know a county sheriff who could swear me in."

Chapter 2

North lowered his right hand, and Sheriff Drake shook it, "Congratulations, Deputy North." The Sheriff dug into a desk drawer and pulled out a six-pointed star badge with the word DEPUTY engraved on it. He handed to Brick, "Now, I'll want that back when we're done."

"I'm not one for souvenirs," he said as he stowed the badge in the pocket of the Mackinaw. "Where do you want me to start?"

Drake pulled a cigarette out of the box on his desk, "You tell me."

"I'll start by going through missing person reports and look for anyone matching our girl's description."

Drake wrinkled his brow and nodded his head, "Good. Let me know if you need any help."

The Livingston County Sheriff's Office was a one-story cinder block building. If one included the restrooms in their count, there were only nine rooms. North dropped his hat on the corner of an empty desk and hung the Mackinaw over the back of the chair. He wandered up to the reception desk, where a middle-aged woman wearing too much makeup and whose sweater was too tight greeted him. She gave North a serious once-over before speaking. "Tom said he was going to swear in a new deputy, but he didn't say how handsome he was. I'm Joyce," she offered her hand.

He gently shook the offered hand, "Rick North, but my friends call me Brick."

"Ooh, I would love to know why," she said coyly.

"Some other time, perhaps. Right now, I'd like to look at any missing persons reports we have here in the county. Probably only need to go back two weeks."

"That'll be easy," Joyce reached into a desk drawer and pulled out a thin Manila folder with the letters 'MP' written on the tab. She handed the folder to North, who fanned through a half-dozen pages.

"This is for the past two weeks?"

"What? No, that's all the open missing person cases we have. Period. Some of them go back several years."

North studied the pages more carefully, "There've been no reports of anyone missing since July?"

Joyce smiled and replied in a snarky voice, "Of course, there have been some reports, but if they're resolved, they aren't in the open case file."

He handed the folder back to her and grabbed a legal pad from a shelf of office supplies before walking back to the desk. North used his pocket knife to sharpen a pencil, picked up the phone, and called for the switchboard, "Hello Brick," Joyce answered, "how can I help?"

"You're the switchboard, as well as the receptionist?"

"And the records and evidence clerk, and whatever else they need me to do. Now, what can I help you with?"

"Looking at the map, it looks like Ingram, Jackson, and Washtenaw counties all abut Livingston county near Hell. Connect me with the Ingram County Sheriff's Office, and we'll check each one for a missing girl resembling our body. Oh, and get me the number for your coroner. What is it, Van Buren?"

"Doctor Von Boren can be reached at SHerwood 9-8191. I'll ring you back when I get the Ingham Sheriff's office." The line disconnected.

North left a message at the coroner's office asking for a photo of the victim he could show around.

In LaSalle Harbor, the phone rang on Barry Tiffin's desk, "Detective Tiffin."

"Barry, it's Doctor Howard. You remember that pin with the red crosses on the white shield surrounded by angels that North gave me a few weeks back?"

With everything that had happened, Tiffin had utterly forgotten about it, "Now that you mention it, yeah, I do. Did your colleague get back to you with an idea of what it represents?"

"Yes, Doctor Bronson tells me that it's the symbol of the 'Equestrian Order of the Holy Sepulcher of Jerusalem.'"

"Whoa, wait, what?"

"He tells me that it's a Roman Catholic organization that raises money for the Holy Lands. I guess it's a pretty hoity-toity group with a well-heeled membership, if you know what I mean."

Tiffin was scratching notes on his pad, "So, rich Catholics ride horses and raise money for Israel?"

"You got me; I'm a Presbyterian," with that, Howard hung up.

Tiffin grabbed North's case notes and began looking for his note regarding the pin.

"Ingram County Sheriff's office," a soft female voice answered, "how may I direct your call?"

"Hello, this is Rick North with the Livingston County Sheriff's Office. Can you put me through to whoever is handling missing persons?"

"One moment, please." North heard the clicking of the call being transferred, "Deputy Kuschel."

"This is Rick North out of Livingston County. Looking to see if you have a missing report on a brunette, twenty to twenty-five, five foot four, maybe a hundred twenty."

North heard the rustling of paper as Kuschel leafed through a file, "Nope, closest I've got is a brunette female, sixteen. Report was filed ten days ago."

"I appreciate your help." North put the receiver back onto the cradle and crossed Ingram County off his list. He picked up the phone and asked Joyce to connect him with Jackson County.

After another unproductive call, Brick set out into Howell to find a place for lunch. He had walked a couple of blocks before he spotted Ralph's Lounge and Package Store. Walking in, he was struck by the smell of stale beer, heating oil, and hamburger grease.

He sat down at the bar and put his worn fedora onto the stool next to his. At eleven in the morning, only one other patron was in the bar, and he was sitting alone in the corner. "What can I do you for?" the bartender asked.

"Beer and a bump," North responded as he looked around the room. There were fourteen bar stools and three tables, each with four chairs. Behind the bar was an assortment of pints and fifths of popular liquor brands.

"Not eatin' today?" the bartender asked as he opened a bottle of Blatz and put it and a four-ounce glass on the bar top, followed by a shot glass filled to overflowing with Canadian Club.

North poured a few ounces of beer into the glass before looking up, "Yeah, no," he answered as he took the shot of whiskey and tipped it back.

The bartender took the shot glass and proceeded to wash it in the sink under the bar top, "You new around here?"

"Make you a deal," North said as he took a sip of the beer, "I'll let you know when I'm looking for conversation." The bartender shook his head and walked away. Before leaving, he purchased a bottle of Old Quaker and stashed it under the seat of the Dodge.

Back in the office, he placed a call to the Sheriff's Office in Washtenaw County. Within moments he was speaking with Deputy Art Chadwick. "When did you say you all found the body?"

"Friday morning," North replied as he lit a Pall Mall.

"We received a report this morning about a missing girl who matches your description."

"That's strange. Why would they wait four days to report someone missing?"

There was a pause as Chadwick looked at the file, "Damn good question. Says she was last seen was on Thursday the tenth."

North took a pull on the cigarette, "And no one thought it was odd? Are you going to be available if I grab a photo we have of our Jane Doe? I can be there in under an hour."

"Yeah, that's good. I've got a decent picture that her fiancé gave us."

North pulled at a loose piece of tobacco that had stuck to his lip, "What's your missing girl's name?"

"Monica Baker. Age twenty-two."

"Thanks. I'll see you shortly." North hung up the phone, pulled on the Mac, and walked to the reception desk, "Okay, Joyce. If the Sheriff wants to know where I am, I'm heading to Ann Arbor. They've got a missing girl down there who matches the description of the body we have here."

She gave him a big smile, "Okay, Brick. Give us a call when you get there."

"Is that normal procedure?"

"Not really. I just want to hear your voice." North could swear that under all that makeup, she was blushing.

He shook his head, crushed the Bradmore onto his mop of hair, and walked out to the pickup. It took almost an hour to make the drive, fight traffic around the University, locate the Sheriff's Office, and find a parking spot.

North stopped at a counter staffed by a very attractive blonde. "May I help you, sir?"

For whatever reason, North felt it necessary to turn on the charm, "I'm here to see Art Chadwick." He casually leaned on the counter, "Can you tell me where I can find him?"

Her breathing became noticeably deeper, "What is this concerning?"

North pulled the Mackinaw back and showed her the Livingston County badge on his belt, "Chadwick's got a missing person, and I have a body that I need to identify."

The blonde stood up. "Let me show you where you can find Art," she said as she led North out of the lobby and down a corridor. He could not help following her hips with his eyes as they walked. "Art, this gentleman says he has a body that might match your missing person." She looked up at North as she turned to go. "If you're looking for a body," she whispered, "give me a call." She was most definitely North's type, tall, buxom, and confident.

Chadwick was a little older than North's thirty-four and was big enough to have been a full-back for the Wolverines. "North, is it?" he asked as he shook Brick's hand, "I'm Art."

"Rick."

Chadwick gave North a quick once over, "Drake loosening the dress code up in Livingston County?"

"Let's just say I'm on special assignment for the Sheriff."

"Come on in and sit down," he directed North to a desk cluttered with file folders, stacks of papers, and an ashtray piled high with filtered cigarette butts. North took off his hat and sat in an offered chair before he pulled a small photo from the Mac's breast pocket.

"Meet Jane Doe," he said as he handed Chadwick the picture.

Chadwick handed North a file with a photo paper-clipped to the front, "Meet Monica Baker."

They each examined the picture they had been handed. "Yup, that's got to be Monica," Chadwick finally said.

North shook a cigarette out of his pack and lit it, "What do you know about the Baker girl?"

"Just turned twenty-two out of Oak Grove. She's a nursing student at the University. Works part-time for a vending machine company. Engaged to a James Withers."

Holding the cigarette between his lips as he wrote, North asked, "Who reported her missing?"

"Withers came in this morning." Chadwick dumped the contents of the ashtray into the wastepaper basket and lit a cigarette himself.

"He didn't notice his fiancée was missing? I find that hard to believe."

"Withers said that she was going home to visit a friend this weekend and didn't think anything was hinky until she wasn't back last night."

"You believe him?"

"Are you crazy?! Of course, I don't believe him. He's got prime suspect written all over him."

North took a deep pull on the Pall Mall, "Any particular reason he's your suspect?"

Chadwick raised an eyebrow as he squinted at North, "It's always the husband or, in this case, the boyfriend. We've just got to pin it to him and make it stick."

"Where's Withers now?"

"Don't worry about him. We know where he works, and we know where he lives. We can pick him up when we need to," Chadwick pushed his chair back from the desk. "Now that we know we're dealing with murder let's go check out Monica's room."

North stood and picked up his hat, "Where did she live?"

"She lived on-campus at the University. The Alice Crocker Hall for Women."

"You sound like you know where you're going, so you drive," North smiled as he pushed the Bradmore onto his head.

Chadwick artfully navigated the sprawling University of Michigan Campus, which North realized was probably the size of the City of LaSalle Harbor. He pulled his tan Dodge in front of the building's Observatory Street entrance.

North looked over the residence hall. A six-story, red brick building with limestone trim. The street level was the second floor of the building and was devoted to a large, well-appointed lobby occupied by several coeds, many of whom turned to watch North in his plaid Mackinaw and Chadwick in his uniform pass.

"Excuse me, ladies," North interrupted a conversation, "can you tell me where to find someone in charge?"

A perky redhead popped up. North suspected she must be a cheerleader by the way she held her arms to her sides as she jumped up from her seat, "The director's office is through the main lounge and to your left. Would you like me to show you the way?"

Chadwick spoke first, "Yeah. That would be great."

She led them away from the lobby, "I'm Kathy, by the way. Kind of the unofficial tour guide of the Alice Crocker Virgin Vault."

North smiled, "Virgin Vault?"

"Oh, sir, this Hall is women only. Some of the Halls are becoming coed by floor, but Alice Crocker will never be swayed by such modern philosophy." The last of this was said in a very stern and officious tone, followed by a giggle. She continued the tour, "On the left are restrooms, cloakrooms, our telephone switchboard, and here is our main lounge; please notice the Italian marble fireplace and the library as you pass," she said with a wave of her hand. "And here is the director's office." She gently knocked on the doorframe, "Mother, are you in?"

A matronly voice beckoned from inside, "Come."

"Mother, these gentlemen wish to speak with you," Kathy said with an exaggerated courtesy.

"Thank you, Kathy. That will be enough."

Kathy turned and called over her shoulder as she bounced away, "It'll never be enough, Mother!"

The director shook her head. "It'll never be enough," she repeated in an exasperated tone. "I'm Mrs. Geddes. Please be seated," she motioned to two floral brocade chairs opposite her desk. "Now, how may I be of assistance?"

North sat with his hat in his lap, "Are you and Kathy related?"

"Oh, heavens, no. All the girls call me Mother. Around here, I have two hundred and forty-eight daughters."

"Ma'am, I'm Deputy Art Chadwick from the Washtenaw County Sheriff's office; this is Deputy North from Livingston. He pulled the photo that Withers had given him from his pocket, "Do you recognize this woman?"

"That's Monica Baker. She's a fourth-year nursing student."

"I have the unfortunate duty to inform you that Miss Baker was found murdered Friday morning in Livingston County." Chadwick and North sat quietly as the director absorbed the information.

"Murdered?"

The two of them let her question go unanswered for a moment before North spoke up, "Yes, ma'am."

"How? When?" the confidence Mrs. Geddes had displayed on their arrival melted into the floorboards.

North continued, "She appears to have been strangled Thursday evening."

"Oh my. The poor child!" a tear rolled down her cheek.

"Did Miss Baker have any relatives? I need to ask that you let us notify them before you do." North searched for an ashtray in the spacious office. None was to be found.

"Monica's father died in the War. The Pacific, I think. Her mother passed from cancer the year that Monica entered the University. She has an aunt in the Upper Peninsula; I'll get you her information."

Chadwick looked up from his notes, "We would also like to see her room. It would be helpful if we could speak with her roommate if that's possible."

"Monica lived in a single, but she was close to a number of the girls. I can arrange to have them chat with you."

"Thank you," North stood, "that will be good. Would you direct us to Miss Baker's room?"

Mrs. Geddes confidence returned, "I'll get her House Director to take you. Men are not allowed to wander the halls of Alice Crocker unattended!" With that, she picked up the telephone on her desk and dialed three digits, "Miss Guinn, would you please come to my office? Thank you," she hung up the phone. "Monica's House Director will be here momentarily."

North and Chadwick sat uncomfortably on chairs that had seemingly been purchased for their looks and not their comfort. There was a knock on the door, "Mother, may I come in?"

Mrs. Geddes, who had been looking through a manila folder that North suspected belonged to Monica Baker, looked up, "Come."

A tall and stunning young woman entered the office. Even with her dark hair twisted into a loose bun, horn-rimmed glasses, and a bulky sweater, her beauty was obvious, "How may I help you, Mother?"

"Gwen, I'm afraid I have some bad news. Monica Baker has been found dead."

The color drained from the young house director's face. North, who had stood on her arrival, guided her to into the chair that he had been occupying, "W-What happened. How did she die?"

Brick took a deep breath. He knew from years of experience that the only way to deliver bad news was to rip the bandage off, "Miss Baker was strangled."

Miss Guinn began to rock forward and back on the brocade chair, "Oh my God, oh my God." Tears flowed down her cheeks.

Chadwick handed her his handkerchief, "Did you know Miss Baker well?"

"I was going to be her maid-of-honor at her wedding next April. She had just gotten her engagement ring from Jim. Monica was going to the jeweler's to pick it up last Thursday from being sized." The deputies looked at each other at the word Thursday.

Mrs. Geddes got up and walked to the chair where Gwen was seated and in an unexpected move, at least to North, knelt and hugged the House Director, "I know this is hard, but do you think you can take the gentlemen up so they can get a look at her room?"

Gwen softly blew her nose before nodding, "Y-Yes," her voice quivered, "I can do that."

The director stood and placed a hand on the younger woman's shoulder, "Why don't you take them up through the freight elevator? That will keep the gossip down, at least for a few minutes."

"Yes, Mother," Gwen answered. "Shall I come back when these gentlemen are finished?"

"Please. We're going to have to meet with all of the girls and tell them what we know. For now, you are dismissed."

Gwen stood and gave the slightest curtsy, "Yes, Mother." She turned to North and Chadwick, "Please follow me." She led them through a sparkling kitchen to the freight elevator near the boiler room. As they stepped into the elevator, she reached up and grabbed a rope that caused the outer doors to close. She then grabbed another rope that brought down a heavy mesh screen. When everything was closed, she pressed the button for the fifth floor. The car stopped at the appointed floor, but instead of lifting the screen to exit, Gwen began to cry. The young woman's shoulders shook heavily with each gasp of air she took between sobs. North turned toward her, and she fell into his arms and cried into his shoulder for a minute before apologizing.

North put his finger under her chin and gently lifted her head until their eyes met, "It's okay to be sad. No apology needed."

"I've never lost a friend before," she sniffed.

North reflected for a moment on the many friends he had lost over the years. "I know it's hard," he put his hands on her shoulders and gave her a look that he hoped would give her strength.

Gwen turned and pulled the mesh screen up and opened the outer doors revealing a commercial laundry room. "This way, gentlemen," she said as she wiped her tears and led them out of the utility area of the building and onto the fifth floor of the residence hall.

"Monica's room is at the end of the corridor," Gwen stifled a sob. Whispering girls appeared in open doors as they passed, "Here we are." She used a master key to unlock the door.

The room reflected an occupant that took her studies seriously. Several anatomical drawings were taped to the walls. On the desk was a stack of books, a small Royal typewriter, and a few trinkets. Above the desk was a narrow shelf with a couple of hats, more books, a photo of a girl, a boy, and a car, along with some letters in open envelopes and a hairbrush. The nightstand acted as a small dresser; its two drawers held sensible lingerie and a floral sachet along with some stationery and several three-cent stamps. The closet had a few dresses, blouses, and skirts. The bed was neatly made; a single stuffed dog kept watch over the room. That was all that was left to say that there ever was a Monica Baker.

North looked at Gwen, "When's the last time you saw Monica?"

"Thursday morning around eleven. She was in a rush to get to her job."

Chadwick and North both grabbed their notepads, "Where did she work?" the Washtenaw deputy asked.

"Monica worked part-time at Canteen, in their office." Both deputies took notes.

"Was she well-liked?" North asked.

Gwen gave a thoughtful nod, "Monica wasn't a social butterfly, but she got along with everyone."

"Tell me about her fiancé."

"Jim's a great guy."

North gave her a long look; a lock of hair had broken loose and was hanging lazily over the corner of her forehead. If anything, it added to her sensuality, "How long has Monica known Jim?"

Gwen looked into North's steel-blue eyes, "I've known her since I moved into Alice Crocker two years ago. She was dating Jim when I met her."

"Did Monica and Withers have any problems?"

"Last Christmas time, she and Jim had a silly spat, and they didn't see each other for almost a month."

North nodded as he made a note in his worn black leather notepad, "Any idea as to what the spat was about?"

"Monica just said that she wanted a different kind of Christmas than Jim did. I didn't ask what she meant."

Chadwick piped in, "Was she seeing Withers exclusively during the time you knew her?"

"She did see one boy when they had broken up. But it was only one date."

North pulled a Pall Mall from the pack and stuck it in the corner of his mouth, "Do you know the boy's name?"

Gwen shook her head, "If she ever told me, I've forgotten."

"Withers the kind of guy that would hold a grudge?" Chadwick asked as North lit his cigarette.

"I should say not. From what I could tell, both Monica and Jim put the whole thing behind them."

North looked into Gwen's moist eyes. This woman was not only gorgeous but confident. Part of him wanted to get to know her better, "In case I need to follow up with you, can I have your phone number?"

A blush appeared on her cheek, "POrter 4-1817." He began to write the number in his notepad when she added, "Gwendolyn Guinn."

"Beautiful name."

"My parents had a thing for the letter G. Dad's name is George; mom is Gladys, and I have three sisters, Gloria, Gail, and Grace."

"No brothers?"

Gwen giggled, the sound of which was spellbinding to North's ears, "No brothers, but the dog's name is Gatsby."

North gave an easy laugh, "Wow."

"You never told me your name," Gwen studied North's eyes.

"Brick, Brick North."

"Your parents called you Brick?" she asked incredulously.

"No, they called me Rick. Brick's a nickname that came along the way."

"I'm Art Chadwick," the Washtenaw deputy interjected. "And we need to get going." He led North back to the freight elevator, "You always on the make, or just when you're in a women's dorm?"

North smiled and pushed his worn Bradmore onto his head, "You've got to admit she's attractive."

"I'll give you that. But if my wife heard me say that, she'd give me something else."

They were both aware of the eyes that followed them as they walked through the lobby and back to the car. "Where to, boss?" North asked as he slammed the passenger door closed.

Chadwick turned the ignition key and pulled away from the dorm, "Let's go talk to the people Monica worked with at Canteen."

The Canteen Corporation was founded in the 1920s in Chicago and had grown into a nationwide vending machine company. From hot coffee to ice cream sandwiches, nearly everything could be purchased from a machine. Many businesses had closed the cafeterias in their office buildings in favor of bank after bank of vending machines.

Canteen in Ann Arbor was located on the southside of town in an industrial neighborhood. North walked in wearing his Mackinaw and

Fedora ahead of Chadwick wearing his sheriff's uniform. An older woman behind the counter looked at North as he walked in, "We're not hiring."

"Good," North pulled the hat off his head, "Who's in charge?"

The woman bristled slightly, "What's this about?"

Chadwick stepped up to the counter, "It's about us speaking with someone about Monica Baker."

"Well, I'd like to speak with someone about Monica Baker, too. She was supposed to be in this morning but didn't even bother to call to say she wasn't coming in."

North opened his worn leather notepad, "When did you last see Miss Baker?"

"Thursday afternoon when she took the deposit to the bank."

"What time did she leave for the bank?"

"It was around two, maybe quarter past." the worker stood.

"Do you know if she made the deposit?" Chadwick queried.

"I checked with the bank Friday morning, and yes, the deposit was made."

Chadwick gave her a quizzical look, "Was there a reason you needed to check with the bank regarding the deposit?"

"You do realize that our deposits are all in coin, don't you? I call every day so that I can adjust our records based on what the bank finds. Sometimes we're a little over, and sometimes we're a little shy."

North pulled a cigarette out of his pocket, "Did she drive or walk to the bank?"

"It's too far to walk. She either drives or catches a ride with one of the drivers." The office worker pushed an ashtray toward North as he clicked his lighter shut.

North shook his head as he absentmindedly picked a piece of tobacco off his lip, "Which was it on Thursday? Did Miss Baker drive, or did she catch a ride?"

"Let me think. Monica drove, I'm certain of it."

Chadwick took up the questioning as North picked a loose piece of tobacco off his lip, "What makes you so certain?"

"I remember she said that after the bank, she was going to the jewelers to pick up her engagement ring. After that, she was going home to spend the weekend with a friend."

"What kind of car does Monica own?" North's pencil hovered over the notepad.

"Blue Mercury. Has a gray fender that Jim, her fiancé, put on after she had a little accident."

"What's the name of the bank she visited?"

"First National on Main."

"And do you know the name of the jeweler she was going to visit?"

"Budd's Jewelers; they're on Washington, a few blocks down from the bank."

For the first time since they'd entered, the woman's voice took an emotional tone, "Is Monica in trouble?"

North nodded his head, "I'm afraid so. Her body was found Friday morning in Livingston County."

She fell back into the chair behind the counter, "Oh my God! What happened?"

Chadwick placed his trooper hat upon his head and straightened it, "That's what we're trying to figure out. May I use your telephone?"

She slid the phone toward the deputy, who dialed his office. "Maureen? This is Art Chadwick. Do me a favor and broadcast an ATL for an older blue Mercury with a grey front fender. If it's located, have them get hold of me. Thank you." He and North took the woman's name and thanked her before leaving the building.

Looking curiously at his counterpart, North asked, "ATL?"

"My boss loves acronyms," Chadwick lit a cigarette, "ATL stands for Attempt to Locate."

The two deputies thanked the office worker and exited the building. North pulled a fresh cigarette out of his pocket and lit it, "We heading to the bank?"

Chadwick nodded before speaking, "You know if you smoked a filter cigarette, you wouldn't always be pulling tobacco off your lips."

"Only dames smoke filtered cigarettes."

"Hey, I smoke filters," Chadwick bristled as North laughed; Chadwick finally laughed too, "Funny North." The Washtenaw deputy found a parking spot near the bank, and they walked through the imposing brass doors, "You better let me do the talking; they might think you're here to rob them."

"Okay, Art. You're in charge," North said as he flicked ash from his cigarette into the ashtray that stood by the counter.

A teller looked up and motioned to them, "I can help you, gentlemen."

"I'm here to verify that a deposit was made last Thursday for the Canteen Company," Chadwick said as he pulled the hat off his head.

The teller looked between the two and smiled, "Let me get the Head Teller, Mr. Fitzpatrick."

North returned the smile, "Thank you."

Moments later, a young man in an off-the-rack pinstriped suit approached the teller window where the deputies stood, "I understand you wish to verify that the Canteen Company made a deposit last Thursday. Is that correct?"

"I'm Deputy Art Chadwick from the Washtenaw County Sheriff's Office," he nodded toward North, "And this is is Deputy North from Livingston County," North nodded. "Yes. We would also like to speak with you about the young woman who made the deposit."

Fitzpatrick excused himself, leaving North and Chadwick to look around the bank. The lobby was busy but quieter than a library. The silence was broken only by the occasional thump of a rubber stamp or clicking of an adding machine. Otherwise, transactions and interactions were completed in whispers.

"Okay, deputies," Fitzpatrick began as he approached, "what would you like to know?"

North spoke first, "What time was the deposit made?"

"Two-twenty."

"And the amount?" Chadwick asked.

Fitzpatrick looked at the ledger in his hands, "Seventy-six dollars and forty cents."

North pulled a cigarette out of his pocket, "Is the teller who took the deposit here?"

Fitzpatrick pointed to the teller with his forehead, "You were just speaking with her. Let me get her for you." He returned moments later, "This is Miss Jennings."

Chadwick and North nodded to her, "You took a deposit from Monica Baker last Thursday, is that correct?"

"Yes. Monica is here almost every afternoon. Is there a problem?" The teller looked nervous.

North took a pull on the Pall Mall, "Was she alone when she came in?"

"Yes."

North blew smoke toward the vaulted ceiling, "Are you certain?"

"I don't remember anyone with her. You can ask Gus; he helped her in with her bag."

Looking around, North asked, "Who's Gus?"

Fitzpatrick answered, "Our security guard." The head teller raised his hand and motioned to the guard who walked over.

"Can I help you, gents?" the guard asked.

North showed Gus the photo of Monica, "Do you remember helping Miss Baker in last Thursday?"

"Oh, sure. Like most days, she came in with a heavy bag of coins. I usually help her when she gets to the door."

Chadwick looked at the guard, "Was she alone last Thursday?"

"I'm positive."

"What makes you positive?" North asked.

"Look, Sonny, I spent thirty-five years as a cop. Just because I'm old doesn't mean I don't see what's happening around me. Now, if we're finished, I have a job to do." With that, the guard turned and returned to his post next to the door.

After getting the names and personal information from the teller and her manager, the deputies turned to leave. The teller spoke up as they were going, "May I ask a question?"

"Of course," North responded.

"Did something happen to Monica?"

North pursed his lips and nodded. The teller gasped, "Is she alright?" North shook his head.

Chapter 3

North looked at Chadwick, "Okay, Art; where's this Budd's Jewelry store?" Chadwick, who was lighting a cigarette, nodded to the right, "Just a couple of blocks up Washington. You up to the walk, or should I bring the car around," he added sarcastically.

North laughed, "A little more training up, and you'll be almost as sarcastic as me." Chadwick joined the laugh, "I've got sarcasm I haven't even begun to use." They walked.

The double doors that opened into the jewelry store were half-inch thick tempered glass, each with two sizeable polished brass hinges on the upper and lower outer corners. In the center were a pair of door handles that resembled diamond engagement rings. Chadwich and North both grabbed a handle and entered side-by-side.

There were two types of stores in the jewelry business, 'guild' stores that sold high-end merchandise to sophisticated buyers and 'borax' shops that sold inexpensive jewelry on credit. Budd's was the latter, catering to blue-collar and office workers. A salesman approached the moment they entered, "Good afternoon, I'm Mr. Nill. How may I help you, gentlemen? Perhaps something for your wives," and then with a wink, "or your girlfriends, maybe?' The salesman added with a chortle.

North looked over the epitome of a sleazy salesman and held the photo of Monica Baker in front of the Nill's eyes, "You recognize this girl?"

"Oh, sure. Her fiancé bought her engagement ring here just a week ago. Mr. Weathers."

"Withers?" North correct.

Nill laughed nervously, "Oh, sure. That's it, Withers. Is there a problem?"

"We understand that the ring was left to be sized. Was it picked up?"

"Let's see," Nill said as he walked them to the back of the store. "Marcia," he said to an attractive woman behind the sales counter, "did the ring for Withers get picked up?" She pulled a drawer open and looked through small manila coin envelopes, each with a name printed across the top.

"I don't see it in the completed work; let me check the logbook." She took a green fabric-covered ledger from a shelf and opened it, "Yes, it was picked up on the tenth and signed for by," she examined the name, "it looks like Monica Baker."

North scratched notes onto his pad, "Do you show a time when it was claimed?"

Marcia put the ledger on the counter and pointed next to the line next to Monica's signature, "October 10, 1957, 2:40 p.m."

"Can you describe the ring?"

The store clerk consulted the ledger for a moment, "One third carat round brilliant solitaire, four-prong head, narrow fourteen karat yellow gold band."

"So, it looks like pretty much every engagement ring," Chadwick said as he lit a smoke. "How much does something like that sell for?"

Nill spoke up, "That was a two hundred dollar ring. They were such a lovely couple that I gave it to them for one and a quarter."

"So," North piped up, "It was a hundred and twenty-five dollar ring." Ignoring Nill's rebuttal, he tipped his hat to the clerk, "You've been very helpful, Miss?"

"Campbell, Marcia Campbell."

On the sidewalk, Chadwick got in another dig, "You forgot to ask her for her phone number, Romeo."

North shook his head as he crushed the Bradmore over his mop of hair, "Gee, didn't know you were keeping score." Then, looking around, adding, "Is there somewhere we can talk through what we've got?"

Chadwick looked down at his uniform, "Well, I can't exactly order a beer dressed like this. Why don't we go back to the office so I can change my clothes."

Back at the Sheriff's Office, Chadwick ducked into the locker room. Five minutes later, he reappeared in casual clothes, "I think I ought to take you to the Library."

The Library was a bar near campus that served cold beer and hard liquor to college kids tired of hitting the books and the people who kept the campus running.

North and Chadwick shooed a couple of kids who sat behind empty beer glasses from a corner table and sat facing the door with their backs against the wall. Within minutes, a beer and a bump appeared in front of each. Art raised the shot glass in a mock toast, "To solving this damn case." They both tossed the whiskey back.

Lighting a Pall Mall, North examined the clientele, which was primarily young men, before looking Chadwick in the eye, "So, Miss Baker takes seventy-five dollars in coin to the bank, deposits it, and goes to pick up her engagement ring."

The deputy nodded, "That's the timeline."

"Then, where's the ring? If she just picked up her engagement ring, shouldn't she be wearing it?"

Chadwick put the beer that he was just about to sip down, "She wasn't wearing it when her body was found?"

"She wasn't wearing much, but she definitely didn't have a ring on her finger."

Picking up the glass, Art took a sip of his beer, "So, whoever killed Monica probably has her ring."

"Or, he pawned it," North observed.

One of the college kids that had left the table for North and Chadwick returned with three friends, "What makes you two think you can just take a table from someone," said one of the friends who was big enough to be an entire defensive line. Chadwick glanced at him; North took a sip of his beer and ignored the question altogether.

"I'm talking to you!" the line said.

North put his beer down, "And we're ignoring you."

"Why don't we step outside?"

North looked at Chadwick, who shook his head, "Nope, don't think we want to step outside."

The big guy laughed toward his friends, "Look, boys, these old men don't want to fight."

"I didn't say I don't want to fight. I said I don't want to step outside," North stood and tossed the Mackinaw onto the chair where he'd been seated before rolling up his sleeves.

"Ooh," the big guy said, "the old man thinks he's tough."

North made a fist and swung it hard into the big guy's solar plexus, causing the abdominal wall to press into his aorta. The young man made a massive grunt as the air in his lungs was pushed out of his body. Stunned, he staggered backward for a second before regaining his balance. The guy brought his fists up and swung a right hook at North, who blocked the punch with his left before sending his right fist into the underside of the younger man's jaw. The big guy crumpled onto the floor.

One of the other young men took a step toward North. Chadwick looked up from his beer, "If you're not tougher than your friend, you're going to end up on the floor next to him."

Taking his eyes off the next young man in line, North turned toward Chadwick, "Come on, Art, don't spoil their fun."

Chadwick stood and took the badge from his pocket, "Probably time for you all to take a hike, and don't forget your pal on the floor." The young men grabbed their friend and made a beeline for the door.

Rolling down his sleeves, North sat down. "Where did you say Monica was going?"

"According to Withers, she was going to Oak Grove."

North shook his head, "Where's Oak Grove?"

"Up the road from Howell in your county."

"Did Withers say who she was going to visit?"

Chadwick pulled the notepad from his pocket and flipped back a couple of pages, "Tara Montrose."

"Did he have an address or number for this Montrose woman?"

"No, just a name."

North copied the information down, "Okay, so she visited the bank, picked up her ring, and then what? I've got a map in my truck; let's get that and plot out the most direct route to Oak Grove."

Back at the Washtenaw Sheriff's Office, North spread the Michigan map across his pickup hood. Chadwick poked his finger at Ann Arbor, "We're here. The easiest route would be U.S. 23 to Michigan 59 to Howell, then Oak Grove Road north."

The sun was beginning to set as North pulled out of Ann Arbor and headed for North's End. He made a quick stop at a drug store before he left the city.

The cat that had been wandering the neighborhood was sitting on the front step when he got out of the Dodge. His instinct was to give the cat the boot. Against his own better judgment, he pushed the door open and let the cat in. North hung his Bradmore and Mac on a peg near the door and visited the bathroom before getting a fire going in the stove. The marmalade-colored cat followed him, purring incessantly and brushing against North's legs. "Okay, cat," he said in an authoritative voice, "if you're staying here, you need to make your own space, and that's not on top of me." The cat blinked and followed North into the kitchen area.

"Hungry, are you, cat?" He reached into a cabinet and pulled out a package of saltines and a paper-wrapped tin of sardines, "Hope you like mustard." North peeled away the wrapper and pried the key off the top of the can. He twisted the tin open and tossed the lid into the sink before grabbing a fork and lifting a fish onto a cracker, which he popped into his mouth. He retrieved the lid and put a couple of sardines on it before placing it on the floor. The cat didn't hesitate and immediately wolfed down the sardines and proceeded to lick the top of the tin, which he pushed around the room.

North poured a couple of fingers of Old Quaker into a jelly jar and sat down at the table. He grabbed the postcard he'd purchased at the drug store and began to write:

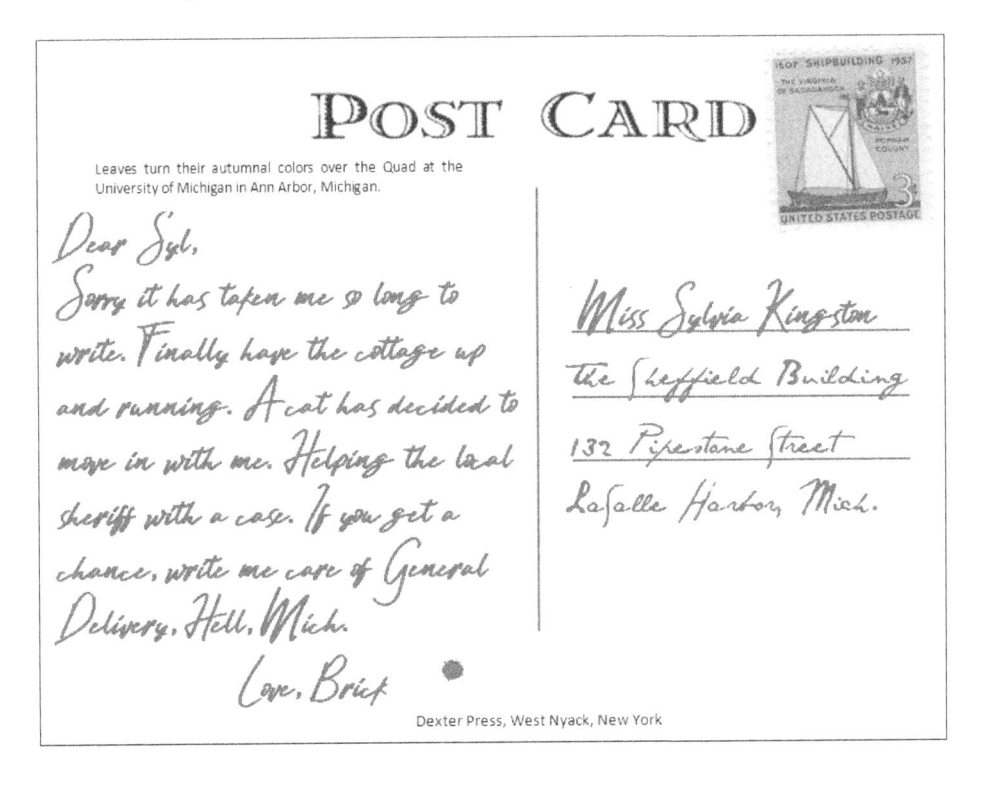

Dear Syl,

Sorry it has taken me so long to write. Finally have the cottage up and running. A cat has decided to move in with me. Helping the local sheriff with a case. If you get a chance, write me care of General Delivery, Hell,

Mich. He hesitated, the pen hanging over the postcard, before he finally wrote, "Love, Brick."

North's first day as a deputy sheriff had been a busy one; he leafed through the "Michigan Daily" he'd bought at the drug store before he and the cat fell asleep in the overstuffed chair.

Brick awoke with a start, sweating hard, his heart pounding within his ribcage. It was all he could do to catch his breath. He brushed the cat off his lap and walked to the sink, where he splashed cold water on his face. The sights and sounds of the Ardenne Forest filled his senses. His field-promotion to Sergeant put him in charge of men whose lives depended upon him following his orders and him sharing those orders precisely. It took fifteen minutes and a shot of bourbon before he finally calmed.

He pulled the cord, lighting the lamp over the sink in the bathroom. It cast more than enough light throughout the cottage for him to navigate and not trip over the cat before he opened the door, "Okay, cat, it's time you and I get some air."

North walked around the lake as far as he could before a creek blocked his path. The cat had wandered off at some point; North neither knew when or cared. He followed the stream, glad that the waning gibbous moon gave him enough light to navigate the terrain. It was close to four o'clock before he finally climbed into bed.

Sunrise came earlier than he would have hoped. He got a fire burning in the stove and set up the percolator before washing up. He pulled on his grey flannel suit and a blue tie, downed the coffee, clipped the badge to his belt, and was at the Livingston County Sheriff's Office by eight. Joyce walked in just behind him, "You dress up nice," she said with a low whistle.

North smiled and tipped his hat, "Thank you. Where can a guy get a plate of breakfast around here?"

Joyce lowered her voice, "You can have breakfast in my kitchen any morning you'd like."

"I'll keep that in mind. Where can I get breakfast this morning?"

"You'll find the Dunn-Wright Diner a block over on Clinton Street; they put out a pretty good meal."

North pushed the Bradmore back onto his head, "If the Sheriff is looking for me, let him know I'll be back in thirty minutes."

"All diners must smell the same," he thought to himself as he settled into a corner booth at the Dunn-Wright and tossed his hat onto the bench next to him.

"What'll it be, hun?" a middle-aged waitress asked as she walked up to the table.

"How's the hash?"

"Greasy, but I think it's decent."

"Great, I'll have the hash, a couple of eggs over hard, toast no butter, and a cup of coffee." As he spoke, he stood and took off his jacket, revealing his worn leather shoulder holster, .38, and the badge on his belt.

"You with the Sheriff's Office?" she asked.

He sat back down, "Helping out at the moment,"

"I give deputies a twenty-five percent discount. I'll pay you to eat here."

North chuckled as he lit a cigarette, "If the greasy hash doesn't kill me, I'll be back." While he waited, he picked up a copy of the Detroit

Free Press that someone had left on the counter. He spent some time reading an article on the Federal Courts delaying Jimmy Hoffa taking over the Teamsters for ten days while the FBI investigated allegations that the election was rigged. "A rigged election, what are the odds?"

"What's that, hun?" the waitress asked as she put a chipped plate in front of him.

"Nothing, just thinking out loud." She refilled his coffee before walking back to the counter.

As was his custom, he finished his breakfast in record time and cleaned the plate with a piece of toast. Folding the paper, he dropped it back onto the counter where he'd found it. "What do I owe you?" he asked as he pulled his change purse from his pocket.

"Buck seventy-five, with the discount, let's call it a buck thirty."

North grabbed four Franklin half-dollars and dropped them into the waitress's waiting hand, "I'll see you again."

"If the hash doesn't kill you," she joked as he crushed the Bradmore onto his head.

Back at the Sheriff's Office, he caught Drake up on the case, "I'm impressed," Drake said as he pulled a cigarette out of the wooden box on his desk, "you've covered some ground. What're your plans for today?"

"I'm going to do my best to track down this Tara Montrose. Don't suppose there's a city directory that covers Oak Grove?"

"Oak Grove can't be seven hundred people; I doubt if Polk could sell enough ads to make a directory worthwhile," Drake referred to the publisher of City Directories for most of the country.

"Well, I'll see if I can come up with a phone number for anyone named Montrose. If I can't, I'll be driving up to Oak Grove."

North grabbed the telephone directory from Joyce's desk and found the seven pages that covered Oak Grove. There were four listings for Montrose. He picked up the receiver and began dialing. He received a busy signal on the first call. No one answered the second number he dialed. He struck paydirt on the third call, "Tara?" a friendly female voice repeated. "That's my niece. She works in town but still lives on my brother's farm."

"Town? What town does she work in?"

"Well, Howell, of course," the tone of her voice caused North to believe she must think him dim.

"Where does your niece work?"

"She works at the diner."

"Diner? Which diner?" North had to pull every answer out of this gal.

"The Dunn-Wright."

"Your niece works at the Dunn-Wright Diner on Clinton Street?" he asked incredulously.

"Yes. Tara cooks breakfast and lunch during the week. They're not real busy on the weekend; well, except for Sunday after church."

North cut her off, "Thank you, ma'am, you've been most accommodating." He grabbed the Bradmore and his jacket and ran past Joyce for the door.

"Where you going in such a hurry?" she called after him, but he didn't pause to answer.

Minutes later, the bell over the door of the Dunn-Wright jingled as he pushed the door open, much to the middle-aged waitress's surprise, "Goodness, you back so soon, hun?"

"Tara Montrose, she works here, is that correct?"

A concerned look washed over her face, "She cooked your hash this morning. Is there a problem?"

"I need to see her for a minute, that's all," North took the hat off his head. "Should I go back to her, or can you bring her out?"

"Tara Beth! Come out here for a minute," the waitress yelled through the service window into the kitchen. A slender, dark-haired girl of about twenty-two pushed her way through the swinging door into the dining room, "What's up?" she asked as she wiped her hands on the soiled apron that was tied about her waist.

"This gentleman has some questions for you," the waitress stepped back but remained in earshot.

"Miss Montrose, I'm Rick North with the Sheriff's Office. I have a couple of questions about Monica Baker."

"Monica! Where has she been? Is she okay?"

"She was found Friday morning down at Hi-Land Lake. I'm sorry to have to tell you that she'd been murdered."

Tara took a step back until her calfs hit the vinyl cushion of a chair; she dropped onto the seat, "Oh my God! W-What happened?"

North pulled up a chair and sat in front of her, "She'd been strangled." He deliberately did not mention the rape. "I understand that she was coming up here to see you. Is that correct?"

"Yes," Tara used the corner of her apron to wipe her eyes. "Jim finally proposed, and she was coming up to show me her ring. Who did this to her?"

"That's what I'm going to find out," North pulled his worn leather notepad out of his pocket, along with a pencil, the pack of Pall Malls, and his Zippo lighter. He lit a cigarette before opening the pad, "How long have you known Miss Baker?"

"We met in grade school; second grade, Miss Kowalska's class. We've been close ever since."

North scratched a few notes onto his pad, "She was driving up here to spend time this past weekend, yes?"

"Yes. Monica doesn't have classes on Friday. She was taking a day off, and we were going to spend the weekend together."

North pulled his handkerchief from his breast pocket and handed it to her, "Where was she supposed to meet you?"

Tara dabbed the inside corner of each eye, "We were going to meet at my parent's house. She always stays with us when she visits."

"What time were you expecting her?"

"Around four o'clock, right after she got done with her work."

North nodded as he made notes, "And what did you do when she didn't show up?"

"Well, I got a little nervous. I can tell you that."

"Did you try to call her?"

Tara shook her head, "We don't have a phone at the farm, and my dad wouldn't let me go to use my aunt's. He said that long-distance calls are too expensive and that Monica probably just changed her mind. Oh my God, poor Jim."

"Were she and Jim getting along? Did you know if they'd been fighting?"

Tara got visibly upset at North's question, "I don't think he'd buy her an engagement ring if they weren't getting along!"

"How would you describe Jim? Is he a pretty steady guy, or is he the type that blows up when he gets upset?"

"Well, Jim has a temper. He and Monica broke up last winter when he accused her of seeing another guy."

"Monica told you that he gets angry; have you ever seen him when he's mad?" North took a drag on the cigarette that had been smoldering in the copper-colored ashtray on the table.

"I've never met him, so I haven't seen him angry. But Monica has said that he can get loud and grabby when he's mad."

North jotted a quick note, "What do you mean, grabby?"

"When she came up here on winter break, she had bruises on her upper arms," Tara pointed at her arm. "I told her that he shouldn't do that, but she said that she had brought it on herself, and it wasn't a big deal."

"Did Monica ever tell you that she was afraid of Withers?"

"Not in so many words, but I gathered that his anger made her feel uncomfortable."

North stood, "I'm sorry for your loss. If you think of anything that might be helpful," he reached for a business card and realized he didn't have any. "If you think of anything that might be helpful, call the Sheriff's Office and ask for me."

Tara handed him back his handkerchief, "North, right?"

"Yes, Rick North," he stuffed the handkerchief into his pant pocket.

Chapter 4

Back at his adopted desk at the Sheriff's Office, North transferred his chicken-scratched notes onto typewritten pages to include in the case file. When he was done, he picked up the phone and called Joyce at the reception desk, "Hey doll, put me through to the Washtenaw Sheriff's Office."

"I'll call you back as soon as I reach them," the phone went dead. He lit a cigarette and waited for the callback. He didn't have to wait long before the phone rang. "Hold for Washtenaw County, Brick." With a couple of clicks, he was connected. The switchboard there connected him with his counterpart, "Art Chadwick."

"Art, it's North. Have you told Withers that Monica is dead?"

"No, I've waited until we knew more," North heard a lighter click shut. "So, what have you got there for me?"

"Pick him up. I tracked down Tara Montrose. She says that Withers can be the jealous type and that he has a temper."

"There's a bad combination. I'll call you when we pick him up. Do you want to be here when we question him?"

"I'll drive down and go with you to pick him up."

Chadwick cut him short, "I think we got it covered."

"Don't get testy, Art. I'm just anxious to move on my case."

"You're case?! I think you're mistaking my case for yours."

North lit a cigarette, "You had yourself a missing person, and that person is no longer missing. I've got a murder investigation, and Mr. Withers has prime suspect written all over him." North took a deep pull on the cigarette, "I'll be there waiting for you to bring Withers in." He hung up the phone, slipped his jacket on, and picked up the Bradmore before shouting into Drake's office, "I'm on my way to Ann Arbor."

While North was on his way to Ann Arbor, Tiffin was still wrapping up the case of the priest, rabbi, and minister who had been brutally murdered.

Tiffin pulled up in front of St. Julian Catholic Church. He and Detective Dan Uher walked up the worn marble steps into the church's vestibule just as the midday Mass ended. Uher made the sign of the cross as they entered. "Let's find Father Novak," he said as he walked up the aisle and past the faithful who were heading to their lunches.

They stepped into the Sanctuary and walked behind the Reredos and into the Sacristy. Father Francis Novak was pulling the fiddle-back chasuble off.

Tiffin startled the priest when they entered, "Good afternoon, Father."

He turned toward the detectives, "Haven't you done enough? April's in jail awaiting trial, and the Bishop has me packing up and sending me to God knows where."

Reaching into his jacket pocket, Tiffin pulled a lapel pin out of his pocket and held it out in an open palm, "You recognize this, Father?"

"Yes, that's a pin for the Equestrian Order of the Holy Sepulchre."

Tiffin looked at the pin and then back to the priest, "You were wearing a pin like this one the first time we met."

"I'm a member of the Order," Novak said defensively.

"May we see your lapel pin?" Uher asked.

Novak blanched, "I-I don't know where it is. I must have lost it."

"We found this one in the trunk of Rabbi Perlmutter's car," the Rabbi had been killed several weeks earlier, and April Cordrey, the woman Father Novak had been seeing, had been arrested for the murder. Tiffin turned to Uher, "You don't suppose the Rabbi was a member of this Catholic group, do you?"

Uher put his hand on his chin and pretended to think for a moment, "The only Jew that I know of who's been involved in the Church founded the Church."

Tiffin stared at Novak for an uncomfortable amount of time before he spoke, "Your girlfriend is awaiting trial for the murder of the rabbi, and it appears your lapel pin ended up in the trunk of his car. Can you think of an explanation because I'm at a loss?"

"April must have found it and had it with her when the rabbi was killed."

"Tell your bishop that you aren't going anywhere until this is cleared up."

"I'm not in a position to tell the bishop anything."

Tiffin pushed the lapel pin back into his pocket, "Have him call me if he has any questions."

Uher turned to Tiffin as they walked out of the church, "You know who St. Julian the Hospitaler is, don't you?"

"Forgive me, Dan. But they didn't teach that when I was preparing for my bar mitzvah."

"Among other things, St. Julian is the patron saint of murderers."

North pulled into the Washtenaw Sheriff's Office's parking lot and ran his fingers through his hair before stepping out of the car and putting his hat on. It had been less than an hour since he'd spoken with his counterpart. He was trying to decide if he should wait with the car or go inside as Chadwick pulled in. He and another uniformed officer stepped out of the Dodge with a tall young man wearing green coveralls.

"That Withers?" North called across the lot.

"It is," Chadwick shouted back. "You want to follow us?"

North pushed himself away from the fender he was leaning on and crushed his cigarette under his foot, "Lead the way."

Chadwick and the other deputy led Withers, who was not handcuffed, into the back of the Sheriff's Office. Once inside, they walked down a corridor and into an interrogation room. The second deputy closed the door behind them and waited outside. Chadwick pointed to a chair in the corner, "Have a seat, Mr. Withers." Withers sat, as did Chadwick. North stood with his back to the opposite corner of the small room.

"You haven't said anything to me since you asked me to come here with you," Wither's tone was a mixture of frustration and fear. "What's going on?"

"My name is North; I'm with the Livingston County Sheriff's Office. Tell me when you last spoke with Miss Baker."

"I've already told this deputy," Withers tilted his head in Chadwick's direction.

Wither looked to Chadwick for help. "Tell me," North said sharply.

"Thursday morning."

North made a note on his pad, "Thursday the tenth, is that right?"

"Yes."

"What time? What time did you see Miss Baker?"

"I don't know. Maybe eight-thirty. I walked Monica from her dorm to the Nursing School."

Chadwick flipped through his notepad, "You told me that it was nine o'clock. Which was it?"

"Eight-thirty or nine. Why does it matter? What's this all about?"

North stepped closer, "You sure you didn't see her later in the day?"

"I'm damn sure!"

Chadwick picked up the ball, "What if I tell you that someone saw you and Monica together after she picked up her ring from Budd's?"

Withers jumped up from the chair, "I'd say they're a damn liar!"

North clicked his Zippo lighter closed, "Sit down! Where were you last Thursday afternoon?"

"I was where I was when the deputies came and picked me up today, Gill Lumber."

North took a drag on the Pall Mall, "What will your coworkers say when we question them? Will anyone tell us that you took a long break or were late returning from lunch?"

Withers was becoming flushed, "No! What the hell is this about?!"

Chadwick spoke quietly and slowly, "I'm sorry to have to tell you that Monica was found murdered last Friday morning."

Withers appeared confused as if he didn't understand what he'd been told, "What?! No! That's not possible. Monica was going to visit her friend. You're wrong. She's still at her friend's house. Did you check with Tara? I bet she's there."

North adopted Chadwick's quiet tone, "I spoke with Miss Montrose this morning. Monica never made it to Oak Grove."

Withers sat shaking his head, "This can't be right. You've got this all mixed up in your heads. That's it; you've made a mistake. You've got to get back out there and find her! If she didn't make it to Oak Grove, she could be lost or been in an accident."

"Jim, listen to me," North said calmly. "Was there anyone that had problems with Monica? Anyone at school or Canteen?"

Looking up at the deputies, North could see that Withers' face was as blank as if someone had erased his emotions, "Problems? No, everyone gets along with Monica. One guy at Canteen got along a little too well. I had to tell him to back off."

North and Chadwick both picked up their notepads. "Who was paying her too much attention?" Chadwick asked.

"I don't know; Cody somebody. He's a route driver. Always trying to get her to go out with him for a drink."

North crushed out his cigarette, "What say you stay here while we check out your alibi?"

Eyes cast down, Withers asked, "Where's Monica now? I want to see her."

"She's with the coroner in Howell. You can see her body when the coroner releases it." North picked up his notepad, pencil, and cigarettes, "Considering she doesn't have any family, you'll probably need to make funeral arrangements for her."

Withers began to sob. Chadwick and North closed the door behind them as they left.

North crushed out his cigarette in an ashtray bolted to the wall, "Where's this Gill Lumber that Withers works at?"

"About two miles away; you want me to drive?" Chadwick joked.

"No," North responded sarcastically, "I'll just wander around Ann Arbor until I find it."

Withers' story checked out; of the eight other employees of the yard, seven of them confirmed that he had been there all day. The eighth had been out Thursday afternoon.

Back in the car, North tossed the Bradmore on the seat between him and Chadwick, "So, shall we see if we can find this Cody guy?"

"Exactly what I had in mind," Chadwick swung the wheel on the Dodge and pulled into traffic on State Street. It took them less than ten minutes to get to the office and warehouse of the Canteen Company. They were greeted by the same older woman whom they had spoken with the day before.

"Well, I must say you're dressed a darn bit better than yesterday," she said as North took the hat off his head, "What can I do for you two today?"

Chadwick flipped his notepad open, "You have a Cody that works here?"

"Yes, he's one of our delivery drivers."

North took the lead, "What's Cody's full name?"

"Dakota White Eagle."

Both deputies took notes, "He's Indian?" North asked.

"Yes, I think so anyway," she said, "what with the name and all."

"Is Cody in today?" Chadwick asked.

"Let me check," the office manager picked up the phone and dialed a number, "Chuck, it's Maxine; is Cody back there? Stop him. There's a couple of men who want to speak with him."

"He was just heading out; he'll be up here in a minute." Precisely one minute later, a tall man with chiseled features walked in through the back door, "I'm Cody. What can I do for you?"

"Cody, I'm Deputy Art Chadwick from the Washtenaw Sheriff's Office," he nodded in North's direction, "and this is Deputy North. We have a couple of questions for you. Is there somewhere private we can talk?"

Maxine pointed to an office, "Mike's not in today. You can use his office."

The deputies led White Eagle to the vacant office. North studied the young man who was twisting his hat nervously, "Sit down." White Eagle did as he was asked, "I'm sure you've heard that Monica Baker was found dead."

"Yes, I've heard."

Chadwick lit a cigarette, "We understand that you've expressed interested in Miss Baker."

"Monica was good-looking and always smiling. So, yes. I asked her out once."

Clicking his lighter shut, North picked up the questioning, "I hear that you pestered Monica for a date. Maybe you got mad that she wasn't interested in you and took your frustration out on her."

The Sioux stood, "Okay, I asked her out a few times, but I never hurt Monica."

"Sit down! Where were you last Thursday afternoon?"

"I was delivering all day," White Eagle took a subdued tone.

"Isn't it possible that during your route, you spotted Monica Baker and followed her?" Chadwick asked. "It seems to me that there was nothing to keep you from taking Miss Baker. There's plenty of room in your delivery van to rape a woman."

"Rape?!" White Eagle's voice became sharp. "I didn't take Monica, I didn't rape her, and I certainly didn't murder her."

North took a pull on his Pall Mall, "Your alibi isn't very tight, mister! No one is going to pay attention to a delivery van if it sits in one spot for a while."

"I covered a rural route last Thursday," White Eagle explained. "During the afternoon, I was in Ypsilanti and didn't return here until after five o'clock. What's more, I can take you to every stop I made. My times are also on my delivery tickets, and you can check with the warehouse manager as to the time I returned."

"We'll give you a chance to show us," North said, mentally crossing White Eagle from his list. The Indian's alibi was just too good to be faked. After reviewing the delivery tickets with the Accounts Billable office and speaking with the warehouse manager, he and Chadwick stepped back out to the Dodge.

"Shit," North said as he slid into the passenger seat, "we're just not getting a break." Chadwick agreed as he put the Dodge into first and pulled back onto the street.

Chapter 5

A white over yellow Chevy BelAir pulled over the pneumatic cord at a Sinclair station just off Route 23, nineteen miles north of Ann Arbor. A young attendant raced from the office to the fuel pumps, "Fill 'er up?"

The driver, a blonde in her late twenties, pulled off her sunglasses and smiled at the attendant, "Yes, Ethyl, please."

"Right away!" the attendant flipped open the fuel door, removed the gas cap, and put the nozzle into the filler-pipe before turning the pump on. He slowly walked by the car's passenger side and took an in-depth look at the driver's legs before walking to the front of the car and opening the hood. He checked the oil and radiator fluid before walking to the driver's door, "Good thing you stopped when you did; your fan belt is cut almost all the way through. You wouldn't have gotten another five miles before it'd broke. The good news is that I'm pretty sure we have one in stock."

"That doesn't seem right! I just got this car from the dealer."

"You can see it for yourself," he said as he opened the car door. The driver stepped out, straightened her royal blue dress, and walked to the front of the car. The attendant pointed to the fan belt next to the generator, "See, it's cut right here."

The driver leaned slightly forward to get a better look, "I don't see it."

He pointed with his right hand and used his left to grab the attractive blonde around the face, covering her mouth, "Shhh, don't yell. This will go much easier if you're quiet." He dragged her into the storeroom behind the office and latched the door before throwing her onto a twin bed that was pushed against the wall.

The driver screamed before being punched in the side of the face knocking her out. The attendant hiked her dress up and cut her underwear with his knife. Somewhat regaining consciousness, she began to scream. He wrapped his thick hands around her throat and began to squeeze. Her struggles added to his excitement, and as the cartilage in her windpipe collapsed, the rush of euphoria returned, this time without the nausea he'd felt before.

He pulled his pants back up before carefully opening the door to the service station's office area. Not seeing anyone, he walked outside, removed the hose from the Chevy, closed the hood of the car, and drove it behind the station. He parked it next to a blue Mercury with a gray fender. He pulled the tall galvanized steel gate closed, which shut out visibility to the yard, before rushing to help a driver that had just pulled in, "Fill 'er up?"

Back at the Sheriff's Office, Chadwick released Withers, "I hope you understand that we had to verify your alibi."

Withers nodded, "I guess. Are you going to talk to the guy at Canteen?"

"We already did, and his alibi is rock-solid."

Withers was visibly shaken, "So, what? Now you stop looking into who killed the woman I loved?"

North shook his head, "No, now we start working even harder. Someone is guilty of Monica's death and that someone will pay." North stuck his hand out and gave Withers' a firm shake.

"Will you let me know when you've found him?"

"Absolutely," Chadwick offered his hand. Then to North, "I'm going to drive him back to the lumber yard."

Lighting a Pall Mall, North tossed the Bradmore onto a desk, "If it's okay, I'll make a phone call from here before heading home."

"Sure, leave a dime when you're done," Chadwick joked as he led Withers out of the squad room and down the corridor. North flipped his worn black leather notepad open and searched for a phone number. Finding it, he picked up the receiver.

"Operator."

"Get me POrter 4-1817."

North replaced the phone in the cradle, smoked his cigarette, and waited for the call. Less than a minute later, the phone rang. "Hold for your call," the operator said.

"This is Brick North. Is this Gwen?"

"Hello! I was wondering if you'd call. Is this about Monica?"

North thought about saying yes, to give himself an excuse for having called, "No, this is personal. I was just wondering if you'd like to grab dinner one of these nights."

"I'm pretty involved with my studies and normally say no to a date. So, I'm a little out of practice. What do you have in mind?"

North pondered the question for a moment, "I don't know Ann Arbor, is there a place where we can get a steak that's quiet enough that we can talk?"

"There's a place called Randolfs. I hear their food is excellent. But, I understand it's expensive."

"I don't mind the price as long as we can talk and get to know each other better." North crushed his cigarette out, "Friday evening work for you?"

"Yes, but it needs to be after six. We have a house meeting that will run until around five, and then I'll need to get ready," there was a girlish lilt to her voice.

"That's fine. Uh, seven okay with you, and where should I pick you up?"

"Seven is fine. Pick me up in front of the Main Library."

"Where is that located?" North asked, his confusion showing.

"When you get on campus, roll down your window and ask anyone you see. They'll direct you."

North liked her confidence, "Great! I'll see you then."

"And don't stand me up!" she chided as she hung up the phone.

North replaced the receiver in the cradle, and with a smile, walked out of the building and got into his pickup. The flathead six engine fired, and he let it warm up a bit before pressing the clutch and shoving the gearshift into first. He stopped at an A&P for a few supplies before pointing the truck toward North's End.

The marmalade cat was waiting at the door when he pulled up the drive, "Well, Mr. Gatto, looking for another handout, are you?" Gatto being the Italian word for a male cat. The cat rubbed against North's legs as he unlocked the door and hit the light switch with his elbow. He placed the grocery bag on the counter, pushed some kindling into the stove, and lit it. After visiting the bathroom, he hung the suit and put on a pair of dungarees and a flannel shirt. North gently pushed the cat, warming itself in front of the stove aside, and placed a couple of split pieces of wood inside the stove. The cat began circling around and between his legs.

North reached into the brown paper sack and pulled out a butcher-paper wrapped steak, a potato, and a can of Puss n' Boots cat food, "I kind of figured you'd be back," he said as he widgeted the can open. Gatto's purring reached a crescendo as North put a small plate of food down on the floor; it continued as the cat ate.

For his part, North put an old cast iron skillet onto the stove and plopped a spoonful of lard into it before dropping in the potato, which he had cut into thin slices. Once the potatoes had browned, he pushed them aside and placed a strip steak next to them in the pan. He watched his Bulova; when thirty seconds had elapsed, he flipped the steak. After applying a liberal amount of salt and pepper and waiting another minute, he slid the steak and potatoes onto a waiting plate.

Gatto took up residence in front of the woodstove and cleaned himself while North ate his dinner, washing it down with a couple of fingers of Old Quaker.

After cleaning his plate and pan, North added more wood to the stove and retreated to the overstuffed chair in the corner of the room. The radio was tuned to WOWO out of Fort Wayne; he listened to familiar music from the forties while his thoughts returned, as they often did, to the men he'd served with and the deaths that so many had encountered.

Tapping on the door brought him to his feet. He picked up the .38, which had been sitting on the table next to his elbow. "Who is it?" he barked at the door.

"Western Union," came the reply.

North carefully opened the door, making sure to keep his sights through the gun. "R. North?" asked the startled youth at the door.

"That's me," North said, relaxing his guard somewhat.

"Telegram," the youth said. He handed the envelope over.

North reached into his pocket and pulled out a dollar coin, which he dropped into the waiting hand, "Gee, thanks, Mister!" North shut the door before tearing the yellow envelope open.

```
533P EST OCT 15 57
HWL243 LASALLE HARBOR MICH 330P EST
MR R NORTH C/O NORTHS END HICKMAN CT HELL
MICH

RECEIVED YOUR CARD GOING ON VISIT TO PARENTS
STOPEVER ANN ARBOR FOR WEEKEND WITH YOU PICK
ME UP AA TRAIN DEPOT
ARRIVE 4PM FRIDAY 18TH LOVE SYL
```

He read the telegram a second time and smiled to himself. He and Sylvia had been seeing each other more and more before he was placed on leave from the LaSalle Harbor PD. A petite blonde, she was not exactly North's type, but he couldn't deny the feelings he had for her, feelings he had for a long while before he finally admitted them to himself. North closed his eyes and pictured how she bounced on the balls of her feet as she walked and the excitement she brought to their time together. Sylvia managed to see light when so often, he could see only the darkness.

He stopped on the last line of the telegram as he reread it, "Friday!" he said aloud. He folded the telegram back into its envelope and made a mental note to call Gwen in the morning.

Sixteen miles east of where North sat, a body wrapped in a bloody sheet was dumped in the bed of a 1953 Ford F-100 pickup. The familiar green and red Sinclair logo was painted on the cream-colored truck doors, which drove south out of Brighton toward Whitmore Lake. If things worked out like they had last Thursday night, he'd find a secluded spot near some vacant vacation homes to hide the body.

Chapter 6

Morning came too early, following a typical sleepless night. Around one o'clock, North had walked to the main road, some two miles from the cottage and back before falling into bed. Gatto had gone with him part of the way before disappearing into the brush.

Seven hours later, Brick was catching Sheriff Drake up on his trip to Ann Arbor when Joyce called from the front desk, "Sheriff, pardon the interruption."

"What's up, Joyce?" Drake asked as he lit a cigarette.

"Got a call from Eberhart Mortuary; they got an unusual question this morning and wanted to tell us about it."

"What kind of question?" Drake asked curtly.

"Some kid wanted to know how long it takes for a body to decompose."

Drake put the cigarette into the ashtray, "Did they mention if it was a phone call or if the kid came in person?"

"He walked in off the street as they were unlocking their doors for the day."

Drake thanked the operator, receptionist, file clerk, and turned to North, "Eberhart Mortuary down in Brighton just had some kid walk in asking about how long it takes for a body to decompose. Why don't you make a road trip and check it out."

North pulled up in front of the Dunn-Wright and stepped inside. He was greeted by the waitress he'd seen the previous morning, "Back for more hash?" she asked as she grabbed a white ceramic mug and filled it with coffee.

"Get me a fried egg cooked hard and a couple of pieces of bacon. Put all that between two pieces of toast and wrap it to go." North said as he lit a cigarette.

"You want a breakfast sandwich?"

"If that's what you call it, then that's what I want."

"You want tomato or anything on it?"

North shook his head, "No, just what I ordered. And no butter on the toast."

"Okay, doll." She took the order that she'd written and put it on a clip over the service window, "Order in," she shouted.

"On it!" came Tara Montrose's reply from the kitchen.

North caught the waitress's eye, "Tara doing okay?"

"I think she's cried out. You catch the guy who did this to her friend?"

Augustine Meijer "Murder in Hell"

"Not yet, but every lead we chase down gets us closer." North turned and looked out the window, "Is there anywhere nearby that I could get a thermos bottle?"

"I've got one back here that someone walked away from some time ago. If you want it, I'll clean it up for you."

"That would be great. How much do you want for it?"

The waitress shrugged, "It's not mine to sell, but I'll make it kind of a permanent loan if you bring it back here for your refills."

"Can't beat that deal." North watched as she pulled a green thermos bottle out from under the counter and carried it into the kitchen. She came out of the kitchen a few minutes later with both the thermos, which she had filled with coffee, and the breakfast sandwich.

He put the sandwich, wrapped in wax paper, and the thermos onto the seat of the pickup; the thermos rolled as he did so. It was only then that he noticed the word BUTCH scratched into the paint. "There's a memory," he thought to himself as he pulled away from the diner.

North usually measured the distance between cities in terms of how many cigarettes it took to get there. Brighton was two smokes away from Howell. He made a stop at a gas station to ask directions; an older man pointed him in the right direction. North found the mortuary and pulled into their parking lot thirty minutes after leaving the office. A small bell above the door jingled, announcing his arrival.

"Good morning, sir," a middle-aged man in a navy blue suit approached. "How may I be of assistance?"

Pulling back his jacket to reveal the six-point badge, "I'm Deputy North with the Sheriff's Office. I understand that someone asked you a pretty strange question this morning."

"Well, yes. I wouldn't have thought much about it, but after reading about that girl who was dumped outside of Hell, I thought it rather odd."

North pulled out his notepad, "Let's start with the basics. What's your name?"

"Robert Eberhart, this is my funeral home."

"What time did you unlock this morning?"

"Right at eight, just like every day."

North scratched on his pad, "And this youth came in right behind you?"

"It couldn't have been more than five minutes after I walked in. Forgive my manners; can I offer you some coffee?"

"No, I'm fine. Thank you. Tell me about the youth. How old would you say he was?"

"The problem with getting older is that everyone looks like they're twelve. But, I'd say that he was probably twenty, maybe twenty-five. Hard to tell."

"Did you get a name?"

"No. Our conversation was pretty short. He asked how long it takes for a body to decompose, and I said there were a lot of variables."

North looked up from his notepad, "That was the whole conversation?"

"No, he asked if it could take six months or more."

"What did you answer?"

"I blew him off and said, 'sure, six months.'"

"Can you describe him?"

Eberhart closed his eyes and thought for a moment, "Maybe six-foot, somewhat muscular, barrel-chested. He had brown hair, crew cut like a lot of the kids are wearing. Looked like he might have played football, you know, thick neck and big hands.

"Any other details you noticed?"

"I guess I've spent too many years looking at bodies, so I notice weird things," Eberhart lit a cigarette, North followed suit. "I'd say he works with his hands, calloused palms, chipped, and dirty fingernails."

"So, a working guy? Does that describe him?"

"Yes, a laborer of some sort."

"What was he wearing?"

"Blue jeans and a tan cotton shirt. Nothing unusual."

North looked out the window toward the parking lot, "You happen to see what he was driving?"

"No, I really didn't give that much attention. Sorry, I know that could have helped."

"Maybe, maybe not. I appreciate the information you did have." North flipped his notepad closed and slipped it and the pencil back into his jacket. Call me if you remember anything else."

"North, right?"

"Yes, Rick North." They shook hands. North walked back out to the pickup and finished the cigarette.

"Who the hell would want to know how long it takes for a body to decompose unless that someone was trying to get rid of a body?" North thought to himself as he climbed back into his pickup. He tossed his fedora onto the bench seat next to him and crushed the cigarette out in the ashtray. Pushing the gearshift into first, he eased the Dodge onto the road and began to search for a payphone.

He found a phone next to an electric horse in front of the IGA grocery in Brighton. He stepped out of the truck and dropped a dime into the phone before dialing the number for the Sheriff's Office. The coin fell into the slot as he dialed the last digit. Joyce answered the phone on the first ring, "Livingston County Sheriff's Department."

"Joyce, it's North; put me through to Sheriff Drake."

"Hey, Brick, I'll connect you in a moment. He'll tell you that the body of a woman was found at Whitmore Lake a few miles south of Brighton this morning."

North held the receiver between his shoulder and his ear as he pulled his notepad from his pocket, "What do we know?"

"Homeowner found the body of a blonde wrapped in a sheet when he went to inspect his summer cottage. She's fresh," Joyce added.

"Do you have an address?" North scratched the information into his pad.

"I'll connect you to the Sheriff," Joyce said before there was a series of clicks.

"Drake."

"Sheriff, it's North. I just finished at the mortuary and have a description of the kid who wanted to know about the dead. Joyce just caught me up on the body found at Whitmore Lake."

"Sounds like the same MO as the case near your place. Young woman raped, strangled, and dropped near a summer cottage."

North lit a Pall Mall, "Is there anyone there now?"

"Von Boran may still be there with the body. One way or the other, Deweiss and another deputy were told to wait there for you."

Back in the pickup, North filled the stainless lid of the thermos with coffee, swallowed the lukewarm liquid, and started the truck, "I know why old Butch left the thermos behind; it doesn't keep anything hot," he mumbled to himself as he swung out onto U.S. 23 toward Whitmore Lake.

The leaves' reds and yellows had given way to brown and bare trees, not that North usually took the time to contemplate the changing of the seasons. Whitmore Lake's cottages resembled those around Hi-Land, one-story clapboard buildings, many of which were constructed with materials taken from demolished buildings. It didn't take him long to find the two Sheriff's vehicles blocking a dead-end lane.

North walked toward the two deputies leaning against one of the cars, "What have we got, Dennis?"

"Oh, hey Brick," the older deputy looked up as North approached, "a cottage owner found a body partially hidden under his front porch near the dead-end this morning

"What makes you think this is related to the body I found last Friday?"

"This body was wrapped in an off-white bed sheet, just like you found. You know the only difference is that a couple of pieces of corrugated roofing were used to cover the body instead of branches."

"Is Von Boren still here?" North lit a cigarette.

Deweiss nodded, "Yes, the ambulance just arrived. It's down there with him now."

North used his head to point to the other deputy, "And who are you?"

"John Majors, sir," the young deputy answered.

"Why are you calling me sir?" North gave him a severe once-over.

Deweiss leaned and stage-whispered into North's ear, "It's the suit. He's never seen a deputy in a suit before."

North chuckled, "At ease, Majors. Hell, I'm newer to the department than you are." Majors visibly relaxed. "Don't suppose the homeowner is still here?"

Deweiss nodded, "Yes, we asked him to wait. He's in the cottage now."

"Which cottage is that?" North said as he looked down the lane.

"Last house on the left. You want to walk down there?" North nodded his agreement as he lit a Pall Mall. Deweiss turned to Majors, "Stay here, and don't let anyone down there."

As they walked, North's head swiveled, his steel-blue eyes taking in every detail. A couple of hundred yards down the lane, North stopped and dropped to one knee. "Dennis, do you remember what the cut in that tire tread looked like down near my place?"

"Sure, it was a pretty distinctive cut."

North pointed to a tire track in the dirt road, "Look at this. Does this look like what you remember?"

"That's it! That's the same tire. Can't be two of them like that," Deweiss grunted his way back up to his feet.

North continued to look carefully at his surroundings; he held up his hand, stopping the deputy, "Look at this tree." He pointed at a broken branch where a vehicle had brushed against it. "What kind of tree is that?"

"We've got one like that in my yard; my wife loves it. That's a flowering dogwood."

North looked around, "It's the only one like it here." He gathered a handful of leaves from under the tree and put them in his jacket pocket.

"What are you going to do with those?" Deweiss asked as they continued down the lane.

North smiled, "Simple, if these tire tracks are from a pickup, as I think they are, some of these leaves might be in the bed of the truck."

"Your mother always said you were smart."

Dr. Von Boren was just zipping the body bag as North and Deweiss stepped up. He paused to let North get a look at the victim, "Don't know if you remember me, Doc, Rick North."

Von Boren shook the offered hand, "Yeah. Good to see you again."

North took a last drag on his cigarette before crushing it out in the moist earth, "What do you know so far?"

"Fully-developed adult female. Twenty-five to thirty. Bruising indicates that she was raped and strangled. I'm pretty sure that her larynx was crushed, just like the Baker woman. I'll know more when I can give a more thorough examination. One other thing, she has an episiotomy scar."

"I'm not quite sure what that means," North looked between Von Boren and Deweiss.

The doctor looked down, "It means that she's had at least one child."

North's face reddened in anger, "Shit. Was she wearing a wedding ring?"

"No, but there's an obvious line on her finger where one has been until recently."

"Thanks, Doc. Let us know what you find."

Von Boren helped the ambulance attendant get the body onto the gurney and rolled into the back of the waiting car. Deweiss pointed to the front door of the cottage, "Let me introduce you to the guy who found her."

The cottage was different than the others around it. Oversized and made of fieldstone and rough-hewn wood. It was more of a rich man's retreat than what North thought of as a cottage. As they approached, a middle-aged man stepped out, "Wondering how much longer I need to be here. The missus is going to be standing on her ear."

"We won't keep you much longer, mister?" North opened his notepad.

"Mitchell, Hal Mitchell."

North looked over the well-groomed man wearing what appeared to be expensive casual clothing and the Lincoln Mark ii in the drive, "Hal, your given name, is it?"

"No, it's Harold, but I never go by it."

"I know you've already answered most of the questions already, but what brought you out here this morning?"

"We closed up the cottage a couple of weeks back, but I had the nagging feeling that I hadn't drained the water from the toilets. Don't want those freezing this winter. Turns out that I had."

North scratched a copy of notes, "Tell me how you discovered the body."

"As I got out of my car, I saw some of the extra roofing material that was used this summer had been moved. Thought some local louts had been messing around. I moved the roofing and found the body. Went inside and called the Sheriff right away."

North didn't like Mitchell; he reminded him of men of money and leisure that sat on Grand Juries, deciding in favor of the wealthy instead of seeking justice. "Do you recognize the deceased?"

"Recognize; why would I recognize her?"

"Just have to ask," North smiled inwardly, knowing he'd upset Mitchell. "May I have a phone number in case we have any additional questions for you?"

"My office number is EXeter 2-3673."

"Thank you. You may leave when you'd like."

Mitchell turned and walked back into the house only to return moments later with a small canvas bag and a tan, red and black plaid jacket. As he walked to the car, North heard the clink of glass against metal, "What's in the bag, Hal?"

"Just some tools I brought to drain the toilet," he said with a nervous edge to his voice.

"You have glass tools, do you?" North asked sarcastically. "Why don't you open the bag and let Deputy Deweiss and me take a look."

Reluctantly, Mitchell put the bag down on the hood of his car and unzipped it. Inside were two bottles of liquor that had previously been opened. Neither bottle had a Michigan tax stamp. "I'm sorry, sir, but you can't travel with these," Deweiss said matter-of-factly. "You can't transport an open bottle of liquor."

"I was going to put them in the trunk," Mitchell said defensively. "I'll just put them back in the cottage then."

Deweiss smiled, "I can't let you do that, sir. These bottles don't have a tax stamp on them."

"That's ridiculous!"

Clicking the lid to his Zippo closed before taking a long drag on his cigarette, North added, "Where did you purchase the alcohol, Hal?"

"Oh, okay; I bought it in Windsor. It's cheaper in Canada."

"And it's also illegal," Deweiss said as he picked up the bottles. "We're going to have to confiscate these."

"Do you know how much that Old Fitzgerald cost?! That's close to a hundred dollars a bottle!"

North smiled, "Do you know what the fine is for bootlegging? I think your lawyer would tell you that it'll be a hell of a lot more than a C-note."

"You haven't heard the last of this!" Mitchell snapped like a man who was used to getting his way.

"You want to call the Feds and report your bootlegging, or do you want me to?" North nonchalantly took another drag on his Pall Mall.

"Fine! Take the booze. Just let me get out of here."

Deweiss tipped his hat, "Thank you for your cooperation."

Mitchell grabbed the nearly empty tool bag and tossed it into the Lincoln before firing it up and backing rapidly out of the drive.

Deweiss looked at the bottles he held in his hands and then to North, "I gather you didn't like Mr. Mitchell."

"I don't like what he represents. Nothing personal."

"How's that?"

"I'm tired of people with money living under a different justice system than the rest of us."

"You remind me of your old man." Deweiss looked at the bottles, "You want to take one of these with you?"

"Hell no. Pour the contents out, take the bottles back to the office, and put it in your report. I don't want anyone saying we stole his illegal booze."

Deweiss nodded his understanding, "Does seem a shame, doesn't it?"

"More than you can know." North adjusted the Bradmore on his head, "I'm going to head back to the office and see if we can find anything on a missing blonde wife and mother."

Chapter 7

North walked into the office in Howell. "Joyce!" he shouted as he stepped through the backdoor and tossed the Bradmore onto his desk. "I'm looking for a missing person report for a blonde, maybe thirty, wife and mother. We have anything here?"

"Nothing here, but we got something in on the telex from Lucas County, Ohio. They're asking us to keep an eye out for a car that was taken for a test drive from a dealer and not returned."

North scowled, "What's that got to do with a missing woman?"

The middle-aged woman gave him a glaring look, "You always this impatient, Brick? If you'd give me a chance, I was going to tell you that it was taken by a blonde that matches the description you gave me."

"Car theft is pretty uncommon for a woman. What does Lucas County know?"

Joyce picked up the sheet of paper torn from the telex, "The dealership said she claimed her name was Helen Tailor."

Clicking his Zippo shut and blowing smoke toward the ceiling, he looked down at the telex, "Who's the investigator in Lucas County?"

"The telex was sent by a Douglas Milner."

North pulled the paper from the receptionist's fingers, "Put me through to this Milner." He paused as he walked to his desk, "And where the hell is Lucas County, Ohio?"

Joyce smiled, "That's Toledo; it's about sixty miles south. Just over the state line."

He stuck the cigarette into the corner of his mouth and walked back toward his desk, "Thanks, doll," he called over his shoulder. He hadn't finished his smoke when the phone rang, "North."

"Hold for Detective Milner." There were a couple of clicks before the line was connected, "Doug Milner, who've I got?"

"This is Richard North. I understand you're seeking a woman who stole a car from a dealer. Do you have a description of her?" North heard the rustle of paper.

"Blonde, petite, maybe a buck twenty, somewhere south of thirty."

"We may have found your girl," North said as he made notes.

"Hey! That's great! I'll start the extradition paperwork. How about the car?"

"Don't worry about extraditing her; she's with our coroner. And I don't know anything about a car. Her body was found near some summer homes this morning."

North heard the distinctive sound of a Zippo lighter being closed, "Dammit!"

North looked up from his notes, "What kind of car are we talking about?"

"It's a nineteen fifty-five Chevy BelAir two-door sedan, white over yellow. Has a dealer plate, DL 9812."

North jotted notes, "Okay, got the plate as Delta Lima nine eight one two. Let me ask you a question. No dealer is going to let a woman buy a car on her own, right? She has to have her husband, father, or someone with her to complete the transaction. How is it that she can get them to give her a car for a test drive?"

Milner chuckled, "Yeah, I asked the car salesman the same thing. He said she was kinda cute and showed a lot of leg. Said she wanted to take the car to show her husband."

"And he just let her drive off?" the incredulous tone in North's voice was unmistakable.

"I'm told she left a hundred dollars in earnest money. The salesman was only thinking about making a sale."

"And they didn't look at her driver's license or anything?"

"No, she gave them a name and address. Told them she'd be back in less than an hour."

North was again making notes, "Did you check out the address?"

"I was born at night, but it wasn't last night," North couldn't tell whether Milner was angry or just being sarcastic. "Two-nineteen Page Street. For your information, that's St. Mary's Church and School."

"So, she's cute and cunning." North thought aloud. "Why would a woman steal a car?"

Milner paused to take a drag on his cigarette, "I've been thinking about that. Maybe she was trying to get away from something."

"Or someone. Do you have a missing person report for a blonde?"

"None that matches her description. And before you ask, I've been checking out families with Tailor's last name spelled like the guy who makes suits and T-A-Y-L-O-R. Came up empty-handed."

"Is the car salesman certain that was how she spelled her name?"

Milner consulted his notes, "The salesman told me that she wrote the information down herself."

"Okay," North thought for a moment, "I'll have our coroner's office mail a photo to you. Gimme a call if anything that comes up on your end."

"And you keep me posted on how the murder investigation goes and if you find out anything about the car."

The two agreed to keep in contact, and North ended the call. He walked into Drake's office and caught him up on the blonde and the missing car. The Sheriff thought for a moment, "A reasonably new two-tone Chevy shouldn't be hard to spot. Most of the vehicles in the county are either older or pickups."

"It could be in Detroit or Chicago by now." North lit a cigarette, "Or tucked into a barn." He paused. "The blonde was coming up from Toledo; what road would she have taken to get up here?"

"The most direct route would be U.S. 23."

"And what route would Monica Baker have taken out of Ann Arbor if she was heading to Oak Grove?"

The Sheriff turned to North, a look of understanding appearing on his face, "U.S. 23."

North crushed out his cigarette in the marble ashtray on the Sheriff's desk, "Then we've got ourselves a connection!"

"So, where you going to start?"

"If it's okay with you, I'll take Deweiss, and we'll look at every shop, garage, barn, storage building, and gas station from here to the county line."

Drake nodded, "That's going to take some time."

"Better than sitting here waiting for the next girl to get raped."

The Sheriff picked up the phone and dialed zero, "Joyce; where's Deweiss right now? Okay, when he checks in, have him return here. I've got an assignment for him." He hung up the phone, "Dennis is down around your part of the woods. Probably won't be back until early afternoon."

North looked at his watch, "Then I'm going to grab some lunch." He picked up his hat, let Joyce know he was out, and walked over to Ralph's where he'd been earlier in the week.

"Hey, the quiet guy is back!" the bartender quipped as North walked in. "Don't tell me, let me remember; you're a beer and a shot of whiskey."

It caught North funny, "You either don't get much business, or you've got a heck of a memory."

The bartender put a small glass and a bottle of Blatz in front of North as he poured a shot of Candian Club, "A little of both." Two men dressed in dungarees and work shirts walked in and sat at a table. The bartender nodded toward North and walked over to take the new customer's order.

North tossed the shot back and began thinking about the two women who had been raped and murdered since his arrival in Hell. They were both younger and attractive. They were both missing after having traveled north. They were... North's attention turned to one of the men who, moments before, had just sat down and was now walking toward him. The man, maybe ten years older than he, gave North a serious look over, "I know you."

North took a sip of his beer, "I doubt that."

"No, I'm serious. 99th Infantry under Major Lauer. You're Sergeant North, right?"

The 99th Infantry Division of the 394th Regiment fought in the Ardenne Forest during the forty-four forty-five winter. It suffered tremendous casualties during that winter but inflicted more upon the German troops. Some members of the Division had been, like North, cut off from the Division and had managed, against the odds, to survive. They later were one of the first divisions to cross the Rhine and began the gruesome task of liberating concentration camps in the Spring of forty-five.

North froze; images of the emaciated prisoners in the Mühldorf concentration camp, some too weak to lift their heads, flooded his mind. The smell of human waste, death, and decay filled his nose, and he choked on the beer he was trying to swallow. He coughed for a moment before managing to say, "Yeah, I'm North. Who are you?"

"Emmett Dolan. You used to call me 'Corporal Emmy.'"

"Emmy!" North stood and extended a hand; it was only then that he saw that instead of a right hand, Dolan had a hook, "Crap, I knew you'd been wounded, but..." He grabbed the offered hook and shook it.

"No worries, Sarge. It got me home," Dolan looked at the suit, "You selling insurance or something?"

North pulled back the jacket to reveal the badge, "No, just helping your local Sheriff."

Dolan sat down next to North at the bar, "You keep in contact with any of the guys from the Division?"

"No. To be honest with you, I try not to think about the war," North topped off his glass with more beer.

"There's a few of us from the 99th around this part of the state. We get together every few months for some beer and a couple of laughs. It would be great if you could join us."

North felt the muscles in his back tensing up as his stomach wound around itself. He tried to keep his eyes focused on the beer, "I try not to think about the war," he uttered through gnashed teeth.

"As a matter-of-fact, we're getting together next Friday night at the bowling alley here in town, and…"

North's voice shook, "Thanks, but I don't need any more reminders of the war. I'm glad to know that you made it home alive."

Dolan got defensive, "Hey, I don't mean anything by it. Just thought you'd like to join us. That's all."

"I appreciate the invitation," North pulled out his wallet and dropped a five-spot on the bar. "Barkeep, this should cover my drinks, and my friend's here as well." He walked toward the door.

"Where are you staying? If you're interested, we can get together and talk," Dolan asked North's back.

Brick stopped at the door, "You know when I think about it, the only thing I'm interested in is to be left alone." The pneumatic door closer didn't allow him to slam the door as he left. He began to walk back to the Sheriff's Office but climbed into the pickup instead. He was stuck between the Ardene and his cottage. Between the war and the peace being alone offered. In his mind, the trees and brush of Livingston County were rapidly giving way to the forests of France. Waves of nausea passed through him, and he began to sweat. North pulled onto the shoulder of the road and opened the door just in time to vomit. He leaned against the open door and tried to catch his breath and calm himself. There was a part of him that knew he needed to be on the job, but that part was shoved into silence by the events of a dozen years past.

Back in the truck and distracted by the voices and visions of the past, North drove through a stop sign and, only through dumb-luck, managed not to be hit by a dump truck carrying a load of gravel. The trucks blaring horn became the sound of a Messerschmitt Bf 109 passing overhead, menacing the line of soldiers he was responsible for.

He woke in the cold, dark cottage having no memory of how he got there, or for that matter, even what day or time it was. Gatto was curled up at his side. He lay there thinking about the encounter at the bar. As so often was the case, people complicated things, and he hated complications.

He pushed Gatto onto the floor and cautiously rolled off the bed. He then realized that he was still fully dressed right down to the Colt under his right arm. "Crap," he muttered as he walked toward the living room and switched on the table lamp. The front door was wide open. He looked at the cat, "So that's how you got in, is it?" He closed the door as Gatto circled between his legs and rubbed against North's calf. "Yeah, I hear you. No need to get pushy," North bent down and scratched the back of the cat's head.

After relieving himself, he poured a shot of bourbon and tossed it back. He poured another shot to sip, opened the refrigerator, and grabbed the can of Puss 'n Boots. He scraped the contents onto the plate he'd been using to feed the cat, "Looks like I either buy more of this, or you find a new meal-ticket, bub." Gatto purred while he ate.

North looked at his watch. It was eleven o'clock. He used the can opener to widget open a can of pork and beans. He ate them cold from the can as he worked on lighting the stove. Noticing he couldn't see his breath, he knew that the cottage was above freezing. But the door had stood open for hours, and it was no warmer inside than it was out. Within twenty minutes, the old flat-topped wood stove had heated the room enough that North was comfortable.

The jelly jar, which served as a glass for his bourbon, sat on the chair's arm as North stared into the darkness through the window. It was going to be a long night.

Chapter 8

Morning came bright and clear. With the living room windows facing west, it wasn't the morning light that woke North, but the room's chill and a full bladder. The cat had pestered him to be let out at some point during the night; he had no idea when.

The empty bottle of Old Quaker explained the headache and dry mouth he was experiencing. He knew the symptoms of a hangover much better than most.

A glass of water, a pot of coffee, and a hot shower relieved many of the symptoms of excessive alcohol consumption. Nausea and irritability were par for the course. After getting dressed, he slung his worn leather holster over his shoulders, swung the cylinder of the Colt open, and spun it. Satisfied that all six rounds were present, he snapped the cylinder closed before slipping the .38 into its home under his arm.

He straightened the worn chenille bedspread and looked around the bedroom before returning to the only other room in the cottage, "Where the hell is my hat?" His voice rattled in his ears. A walk to the pickup and a look into the cab proved as fruitless as his search of the house; his old Bradmore fedora was not there either. "Shit!" He dug around in his pockets, found his keyring, and locked up before getting the Dodge warmed up.

Fifteen minutes later, he was walking into the Livingston County Sheriff's Office, "The Sheriff wants to see you," Joyce called out as the door clicked shut.

North walked past her and toward Drake's office, "Yeah, I bet he does."

Sheriff Drake looked up from his desk, "What happened to you yesterday?! I had Deweiss sitting here on his ass for almost two hours before I sent him back out!"

"Yeah, sorry about that. I wasn't feeling too well after lunch and went home."

Drake gave him a severe look over, "You look like hell."

"Funny, that's exactly how I feel."

"Can I offer you the hair of the dog? You may not believe this, but I recognize a hangover when I see one." Drake pulled a bottle of scotch from his desk drawer.

North put a hand up, "I think I'll pass. Any chance I can get Deweiss to start the search with me this morning?"

"He'll be in shortly. I think this may be a wild goose chase. Those cars could be halfway across the country by now." He opened the cigarette box on his desk and pulled one out.

North took a Pall Mall from his pocket and lit it from the lighter that the Sheriff held out, "It's better than waiting for something to happen. In the meantime, we might turn up other criminal activity that may be flying under the radar."

Deweiss strolled in as North looked over the case files of both murdered women, "What happened to you yesterday?"

"Wasn't feeling well yesterday afternoon," North answered defensively.

"Yeah, from the looks of you, I'd say that you don't feel well today, either."

"You remember my mother?"

Deweiss nodded, "Nora? Of course, I remember your mother. Why?"

North stood, "Good, you know I had one, and I sure as hell don't need another. Now, you ready to go looking for our missing cars?"

"Sure thing, I need to see a man about a dog before we go," the deputy walked in the direction of the men's room.

Once in Deweiss' radio car, they headed out Grand River Road toward U.S. 23. "Where's your hat?"

"Damned if I know," North pointed to a group of abandoned-looking Quonset huts off to the south of the road, "Let's take a look over there." The Deputy dutifully drove toward the buildings. They exited the car and approached the building closest to the street. North used the side of his hand to wipe dirt off a window and look inside. Deweiss did the same thing at a second building. "Don't see much of anything, certainly don't see two cars," North called out.

"Yeah, nothing here. Let's look in the third building," Deweiss was moving quicker than North thought possible for a man of his age.

There were no windows on the third Quanset. Deweiss and North pulled at the sliding double doors; they were securely chained shut, "Without a search warrant, we're not getting in there," Deweiss offered.

"From the looks of the weeds grown up in front of these doors, it's been a long time since anyone was in there. Let's move on."

The two checked out a few dozen buildings and properties throughout the morning. It was approaching noon as they pulled into a Sinclair gas station. The bell called out two clear rings as their car passed over the pneumatic cord. They parked in front of the station's office. A good-sized young man dressed in cream-colored slacks and shirt with a matching campaign hat walked out of the building, "Help you?"

Deweiss tipped his trooper hat, "Just want to take a look around. What's behind that metal fence behind the station?"

The attendant became noticeably nervous, "Nothing, really. Just a couple of old junkers and worn tires."

North lit a cigarette, "You wouldn't mind if we just took a quick look, would you?" It was more of a statement than a question.

Looking between North and Deweiss, the young man shook his head, "No, sure, that's alright. Just let me get the key to the padlock." He began to turn toward the office door before he took off at a dead run. Still working off his hangover, North paused for just a second before he was on the youth's heel. "Dennis, find a phone and call this in!" He shouted over his shoulder.

A block away, the attendant ran around the side of a tackle shop. North had just made the turn when a two-by-four struck him in the middle and sent him reeling back before he crashed onto his butt. The youth began to approach with the piece of lumber held over his head as North drew the Colt from under his arm, "Drop it, or it'll be the last thing you ever do." The attendant stepped toward North, who fired once, striking the youth just under the right arm. The two-by-four fell to the ground. The young man dropped to his knees and screamed in pain.

"I told you to drop the board. And shut up, that bullet went through and through. You're not hurt that badly." North grabbed his handcuffs and bound the youth's arms behind his back before helping to pull him to his feet. "Let's find out exactly what you didn't want us to see." He pushed the young man ahead of him, Colt at the ready.

Minutes later, they were back at the service station. "You alright?" Deweiss called out as they approached.

"Yeah, we're good," blood soaked through the youth's cream-colored shirt.

"Looks like your friend there got hurt. Should I call for an ambulance?"

"Nah, he's fine," he looked at the attendant, "aren't you?"

"You tried to kill me!"

"If I had wanted to kill you, you wouldn't be standing here, bellyaching! Now, where's the key to the fence?"

The youth nodded toward the desk in the office, "It's in the top drawer."

Deweiss went in while North kept a hand firmly clasped around the youth's left arm. Returning with a ring of keys, North and the kid followed Deweiss, who found the key for the large Yale padlock that held the fence closed. He pulled the gate open. There were several old cars, a pile of tires, old oil drums, and six healthy marijuana plants under a transparent Visqueen awning against the building's back. "Well, look what we have here," North quipped as he pushed the youth forward, "I suppose you're going to tell me you don't know anything about these."

The youth looked down, "They're not mine."

"Look at this, North," Deweiss was pushing his way through the six-foot plants. "He's got these tucked next to a vent blowing hot air out of the back of the garage."

"Are you going to arrest me?"

"No, I'm not going to arrest you," North said as he lit a cigarette. The youth suddenly relaxed. "The State Police, however, will arrest you for violation of the Federal Narcotic Control Act."

The young man slumped, "What's that going to cost me?"

North took a draw on his cigarette, "I don't rightly know. Simple possession carries a sentence of two to ten years and a two thousand dollar fine. But this isn't simple possession, is it?"

They called both the State Police and an ambulance from the office of the service station. The State boys based out of Post 12 in Brighton arrived before the ambulance did. "How much giggle-weed did you boys find?" asked the first Trooper.

"Well, I'll let you take a look for yourself. I'd say enough to make a small town happy." North led them behind the station.

"Holy smokes," the Trooper took off his hat and scratched the back of his head. "That's an understatement. Has your boy told you who he's working with? This is too much for one punk gas station attendant to distribute."

"Other than asking for medical attention, he's been pretty quiet. I'll leave it to you to figure out what he's up to." By the time they'd walked to the front of the building, the ambulance had arrived.

"How's our offender?" the Trooper called out to one of the ambulance workers.

"The bullet went through the *latissimus dorsi*," seeing the blank look on the troopers face, he added, "the meat under his arm. There's no reason for us to take him to the hospital. We bandaged him up."

"Great, then he can make it back to the Post." The Trooper turned and shook North's hand. "Good work, deputy."

It was pushing one o'clock before North and Deweiss were back in the car, "Where to next, Rick?"

"Why don't we head back to Howell? I could use some lunch."

"Works for me," Dennis said, adding, "I think I'll go home and check on the missus while you're having lunch."

"The missus?" North looked in his direction, "Something wrong with your wife?"

"I don't talk much about it, but yeah, she's a pretty sick gal." North saw Deweiss turn inward. "She's been fighting colon cancer, and it's been rough on her. She had surgery three weeks ago, and I have to change her bag for her."

"Oh man, Dennis, that's got to be hard on both of you."

"You ever been married?"

"No, I haven't," North lit a Pall Mall.

"Then you wouldn't understand. The sacrifices we make in marriage are a large part of what holds us together."

Twenty minutes later, Deweiss stopped the car in front of Ralph's Lounge. "You want me to pick you up here or back at the office?"

North stepped out of the Dodge and onto the sidewalk, "At the office is good, thanks." He closed the door as the car pulled away from the curb.

He had just walked inside when the bartender called out, "Came back for it, did you?"

"What's that?" North asked as he parked himself on a stool at the bar.

"Your hat. You left it on the stool next to where you were sitting when you ran out of here yesterday." He put the Bradmore and a bottle of beer on the counter. North placed the hat on the barstool next to the one he occupied and took a deep drink of the beer as he waited for the shot of whiskey to be poured. "You left here in kind of a hurry yesterday."

North tossed the offered shot back, "What's it to you?"

"I've known Emmett Dolan for some ten years. He's dealt better with the wounds he received in the war than you have. At least from your reaction yesterday."

The muscles between North's shoulders and those in his neck tightened; he felt anger building in his gut. "The wounds I got in the War healed just fine," he fought to keep his voice level, but he nearly shouted the words across the bar.

The bartender poured another shot. This one, he swallowed himself, "Not all of our wounds could be treated with sulfa, gauze, and bandages."

The lid to the Zippo clicked shut; North took a deep pull on a cigarette, "What're you talking about?"

"I'm just saying that some of the scars we came home with aren't the kind that can be seen. Some of us wear our scars up here," The bartender pointed at his own head.

"What would you know about it?"

"Let's just say that I recognize the scars that you're carrying as ones that I have too. I have vivid memories of events that happened years ago that seem like they're happening now. Sometimes, I try not to fall asleep because I'm afraid of waking up still trapped in the bowels of the Oklahoma after she capsized in Pearl Harbor. Three mates and I were in a compartment for almost two days before we were rescued."

North sucked on the beer, "That's too bad, but I don't think you and I have anything in common."

"Let me see if I got this right: you sleep too little, drink too much, can't keep a relationship, you're hyper-alert, easily startled, and somehow your life is so fucking wonderful that you ended up here in Podunk working for the sheriff."

Brick paused, the bottle of beer suspended between the counter and his lips. He'd worked hard over the years not to talk about this as he was certain no one would understand. "I lost a lot of friends, saw a lot of terrible things."

"Four hundred twenty-nine men died when the Japanese attacked the Oklahoma. Sometimes when I lay down, I can hear the screams of men who had lost limbs or had their guts spread across the deck, echoing through the metal corridors of a dying ship. We all lost friends, and many of us came home wondering why we lived, and they didn't."

"I came for a drink, not a headshrinker."

"Look, I see a lot of guys come through here. If I'm honest, most of those who come in aren't happy. Some hate their wives, some their bosses, and some their pasts. I've gotten pretty good at recognizing which is which."

North finished the beer, took two dollars out of his pocket, and tossed them on the bar, "You have no idea what you're talking about. There's nothing wrong with me." He stood, started toward the door, and turned back to grab the Bradmore.

The bartender grabbed a rag and wiped the counter where North had been seated, "Maybe I do, maybe I don't. That's for you to decide. If you want to talk, you know where I'm at."

"Yeah, whatever." North walked through the door and turned toward the Sheriff's office. "He doesn't know shit about me," he said loud enough that a woman across the street turned and ducked into a store. A strange feeling washed over him as he walked. It was a mixture of confusion and relaxation, insecurity and vulnerability, hope and betrayal. Overwhelmed, he sat down on a park bench. A honking horn brought him out of his thoughts.

"There you are!" Dennis Deweiss called out from the brown and white Dodge, "I've been looking all over for you."

"Guess I got lost in my thoughts," North climbed into the Sheriff's vehicle. "Where to next?"

"Let's start where we stopped," Deweiss depressed the clutch, pushed the gear shift into first, and headed back out of town. "I see you found your hat."

North looked out the window, "How's that?"

"Your hat. You found your hat."

"Oh, yeah."

The older deputy looked over toward North, "You seem pretty distracted. You okay?"

"Me? Yeah, I'm fine. Just got a lot on my mind."

Deweiss smiled, "I don't doubt that, what with your lady friend coming in tomorrow. What time is she coming in?"

"Four."

"You going to spend time in Ann Arbor? Michigan is playing Northwestern. Maybe you two can take in the game. It's Homecoming, but I bet you can still get tickets." Deweiss turned the car onto the main road out of Howell. Fifteen minutes later, they were pulling into a farmyard. There hadn't been any conversation between the two men. "What say you check out that barn? I'll go look behind those outbuildings."

North, who had been daydreaming about the troop-carrier that had brought him back stateside after the War, startled at Deweiss' comment. "What? Oh, yeah, sure."

They had just exited the car when a middle-aged man in bib-overalls came trotted up to them from the house, "Can I help you, gents?"

"Looking for a couple of missing cars," North shouted over the roof of the Dodge. "You don't mind if we take a look around, do you?" The last was more of a statement than a question.

"Don't mind at all. What makes you think you'll find them here?"

Deweiss walked toward the farmer, "We're checking about everywhere along the main drag where someone could stash a couple of cars. Nothing personal."

Five minutes later, Deweiss waved at the farmer as they pulled out. North lit a cigarette and opened the vent window so he could flick ashes out, "Well, that's another one down. My gut says we're not going to find the cars in a farm building. Why would a woman need to stop if she was driving?"

The deputy gave North a nod, "I think you're on to something there. She might want something to eat or use the lady's room."

"Or get gas," North said through the cloud of cigarette smoke that he exhaled. "The Baker girl leaves Ann Arbor to go home for the weekend. Make's sense she might need to put a few gallons in the tank. And cars on dealer lots never have much gas in them, so the Tailor woman probably would have needed gas."

"Gas stations it is!" Deweiss drove toward Brighton. "I'd appreciate it if we can quit about three. Wilma, the missus, wasn't feeling all that good when I was home. If we cut off about three, I can be home with her by four."

"Yeah, sure." North honestly wondered if he had it within himself to care as deeply for someone as Deweiss did.

Chapter 9

In LaSalle Harbor, Barry Tiffin was going through the notes that he and North had written regarding the murders of Monsignor Kelsey, Rabbi Perlmutter, and Pastor Mullins. They had April Cordrey and her brother Russell sitting in the County Jail awaiting trial for the murders. But, truth be told, he still wasn't convinced the young priest who was having an affair with the Cordrey woman wasn't somehow involved.

"Tiffin!" Pete Cummings, the Chief of Police, shouted across the squad room. "What're you working on?"

Closing the file and slipping it under the blotter on his desk, Tiffin turned to look at his boss, "Just pulling some loose threads together."

"Where's Uher?"

"He's not in yet."

"I can see that! Any idea if he's planning to grace us with his presence?" The tone in Cummings voice revealed more anger than sarcasm.

Tiffin lowered his voice, "You know that he's been having some problems at home. I think he's flopping on a friend's sofa."

"I don't care if he's sleeping in the damned Lincoln bedroom! Unless he wants to get demoted to graveyards on Port Patrol, he needs to be in on time!"

Uher had just walked into the squad room as Cummings was finishing his rant. "Sorry, Chief. I had a problem getting the car started."

"I just promoted Detective Tiffin here to be your nanny. He's going to see that you're here on time. And if you're not, it's on his ass. Now, you two get yourselves over to Memorial Hospital. There's a girl there who's been attacked. Find out what you can, but take it easy on her. She's just fifteen."

Flipping his notepad open and shaking his head, Tiffin asked, "Crap, what's her name?"

"Linda Allison. You'll find her in the Emergency Room."

Dan Uher looked between the chief and Tiffin, "Allison, like Mayor Allison?"

Cummings looked between his two detectives, "His daughter. I don't need to tell you that we want to get this taken care of quickly and quietly."

Tiffin phoned dispatch before he and Uher grabbed the Ford Mainline the Detective Unit shared from the motor pool. Uher slid into the passenger seat as the car lurched toward Main Street, "What does the boss mean that you're going to be my nanny?"

"He means that if you're late, I'm in trouble." He steered the car down Colfax toward Napier Avenue and the hospital.

Uher lit a cigarette, "And shit rolls downhill."

"Yes, it does. Look, I just found out that my wife's expecting our third. I don't need you doing anything that'll screw up my job."

"Got a bun in the oven? That's great!"

"Just remember, if you lose me, my job, Kaye, the kids, and I are moving in with you." Tiffin turned the dark blue Ford into the Emergency Room entrance, "Let's check on Miss Allison."

A flash of the badge got the detectives admitted through the double doors that led to the treatment bays. Uher got the attention of a young nurse, "Looking for the Allison girl." The nurse nodded to the last curtained-off area at the end of the corridor, "Miss Allison is in bed four. Her parents are with her now."

Tiffin gave the nurse a concerned look, "Is she okay?"

The nurse shook her head and lowered her voice, "She's pretty banged up physically. Looks like she was used as a punching bag, and she was assaulted, uh, sexually. I'm more concerned about her emotionally. She hasn't said two words since she was brought in."

Tiffin thanked the nurse, and they walked toward the treatment area to which they had been directed. Uher was just reaching for the curtain when it slid back. Mayor Allison stepped out, "You two detectives?"

"Yes, sir. I'm Detective Tiffin…"

The mayor cut him off, "I don't give a shit who you are. The question is, who called you?"

Tiffin took a moment to let the temperature of his blood drop a couple of degrees, "It's protocol for the hospital to notify the police department when someone is brought in as your daughter was."

Allison leaned forward and lowered his voice, "You tell Cummings that if he wants to keep his job, he'll keep you away from my family."

"Mr. Mayor, someone hurt your daughter. We want to be able to make certain that whoever it was, doesn't hurt anyone else," Uher offered.

"I take care of my family. I don't need help from Frank and Joe or whoever you are."

Tiffin stretched to his full five-foot-ten, "If you know who did this, you need to tell us. You can't take the law into your own hands."

"And you aren't in a position to tell me what to do. Now go back and tell Cummings what I told you. And if I find you sniffing around where you don't belong, I will fire you. You can take that to the bank." Allison turned on his heel and walked back through the curtains and to his daughter and wife.

Tiffin pushed the notepad he'd been holding into his jacket pocket and made his way to the exit with Uher in tow.

Back in the morning sun, Uher finally felt comfortable enough to speak, "Frank and Joe? Who the hell are Frank and Joe?"

Tiffin lit a cigarette, "The Hardy Boys. His honor, the Mayor, attempted to insult us."

Uher bummed a cigarette from Tiffin, "Well, comparing us to a couple of teenage detectives sounds pretty insulting to me."

"You and he are missing a major point," Tiffin smiled as he stepped into the car.

"Oh yeah, what's that?"

"The Hardy Boys always solved the crime."

Uher laughed, "So which one am I, Frank or Joe?"

"You're the one that always gets to work on time."

Chapter 10

Deweiss checked his watch as he and North left the third service station on their list. It was almost three o'clock; there was one more station to look into, "If it's okay with you, can we look into this last one in the morning? I should be getting back to Wilma."

"Sure, I'll run you back to Howell. I might come back down here and check out that last station on my own. What did you say the name of it was?"

"Pacek Sinclair," Deweiss said as he looked up from his notebook.

"Paycheck, like what you get on Fridays?" North asked as Deweiss wheeled the car back onto the main road.

"Right pronunciation, wrong spelling. It's P-A-C-E-K."

North nodded, "Besides, if I check it out myself, I can free up some time tomorrow morning to get ready for Sylvia."

"Sylvia? That's the name of your ladyfriend?" Deweiss asked as the countryside, grayer than the imposing sky, rushed past the windows.

"I guess I never mentioned it. But, yeah, Sylvia Kingston."

"You must be sweet on her to invite her up here."

"Well, if you must know, she invited herself."

"Times have sure changed since I was dating. Back in my day, a girl would have never invited herself to spend the weekend with a man."

North chuckled to himself, "Girls probably had to ride on a buckboard back in your day."

"I'm from your parent's generation. I don't imagine they would have liked that reference."

"Ha, shows what you know," North finished lighting a cigarette off the butt of the one he'd been smoking, "My father said he just grabbed my mother by the hair and dragged her back to his cave."

"Nora would have torn your dad's arm off if he'd tried that."

North took a deep pull on the Pall Mall, "And beaten him with it, too."

The trip back into Howell took less than twenty minutes. North took a few moments to update the Sheriff and the case file that he was building. He had just pushed the Bradmore onto his head and was heading to the door when Joyce called out from the front desk, "You still here, Brick?"

"Just leaving." He called as he walked toward the backdoor and the parking lot where his pickup was parked.

"I think you better come up here."

He turned and walked up to the front desk. On the other side was a man and woman, both visibly upset. Joyce spoke up, "This is Mr. and Mrs. Kaiser, their daughter, Margaret, hasn't been seen since last night."

North shook his head as he pulled the swinging gate next to the front desk inward, "Folks, I'm Detective," he paused for a moment, "Deputy North. Why don't you come in and let's get some more information." He led the couple to his desk and pulled a couple of chairs up. "How old is your daughter?" he asked as he opened his notepad.

"Seventeen," Mr. Kaiser said as his wife gently blew her nose into a lace handkerchief.

"And your first name, sir?"

"Charles and this is my wife, Iota."

"Thank you, and Margaret is your daughter's name?"

"Yes, that's correct, but everyone calls her Maggie."

"When did you last see Maggie?"

"Last night, right after supper," Mrs. Kaiser said softly.

"Was she by herself when she left," North held the pencil over his notepad as he awaited the answer.

"No," Iota's voice was barely above a whisper, "Maggie was with that Peters boy, Jason."

"Have you been in touch with Jason's parents? Have they seen Maggie?"

Mr. Kaiser spoke up, "Yes, we called them. They haven't seen Maggie or Jason for that matter."

"Excuse me just a moment," North pushed himself away from his desk and walked up to Joyce, where he quietly said, "Call over to the Court House. See if Jason Peters and Margaret Kaiser applied for a marriage license." Joyce nodded and pushed a quarter-inch jack into the switchboard behind her desk. North walked back to the Kaisers, "I'm having our receptionist follow-up on a hunch." He had just sat down when the phone rang, "North. Uh-huh, when? Okay, thank you." He replaced the handset on the cradle before looking at the couple staring at him.

Mr. Kaiser finally said, "Well?"

"Well, Judge Williamson married your daughter and Jason at noon today in his courtroom."

Kaiser jumped to his feet, "What?! That's ridiculous; they can't get married. She's only seventeen."

"How old is the Peters boy?" North lit a Pall Mall and took a deep drag.

"He's nineteen, but that's not the point!"

"They are both above the legal age of consent. According to the State, they have every right to be married. Maggie didn't need your consent." North blew smoke toward the ceiling.

The wooden desk chair fell over as Mr. Kaiser jumped to his feet, "I'll kill him!"

North rose and looked down at the redfaced man, "No. You won't. Why don't you and your wife go home and figure out how you're going to make nice with your new son-in-law and his family." The couple left, with Mr. Kaiser sputtering and his missus sobbing.

North followed them to the Sheriff's Office's front door, then turned to Joyce, "There goes another happy family."

"You ever been married, Brick?

If it was possible to smile sarcastically, North did so, "And there goes a prime example of why I'm not." He looked at the clock; it was past four. "I thought about going back down to Brighton; I have one more service station to check. Getting a little late to do that now. Guess I'll head out."

Joyce gave him a smile, "Have any plans for the evening?"

"I've got a little shopping to do," North pushed the fedora onto his head.

Joyce leaned forward and, with her elbows on the desk, placed her chin against the back of her hands, "I'm a size eight if you're shopping."

North chuckled, "Well, you are smaller than me."

"What's that supposed to mean?"

"My father always said never buy clothing for a woman who's as big as you are."

"What? Why's that?"

"So the clerk wouldn't think it's for me."

"Oh! You're terrible!" Joyce laughed, then, in a flirty voice, added, "That offer for breakfast at my place is still open."

"I appreciate that. Have a good night." North turned and walked toward the backdoor and the parking lot. Joyce shrugged and turned back to her typewriter.

Once in the pickup, North headed for Huneryager's, the general mercantile that the locals referred to as "Honey Acres." He purchased some new sheets and pillowcases and a couple of thick bath towels to replace the cottage's threadbare linens. His next stop was O'Brian's

Market, where he stocked up on food that could be easily prepared in the limited kitchen he had, along with several cans of cat food. Stopping at the florist, he picked up a small bouquet before making a quick trip through Ralph's for a bottle of Chianti and one of Old Quaker. He was pleased that the bartender was nowhere to be seen. His shopping done, he was on the road back to North's End. The sun had set by the time he pulled up next to the cottage. Gatto was waiting at the door. North pushed the door open, and the cat made a beeline for the place where his plate would soon be. "You're as punctual as clockwork," North chided. "Well, you're going to have to wait."

Groceries put away, clothes changed, and three fingers of bourbon in a glass, North finally opened a can of Puss 'n Boots and fed Gatto before slicing a couple of slices of bread and a thick slab of braunschweiger for himself. "Onion!" he thought to himself, "I should have grabbed an onion to go with this."

North cleaned the cottage while the cat cleaned himself in front of the stove. The old radio on the kitchen counter pumped out Country and Western songs as he cleaned the bathroom and straightened the bedroom. He looked at the new linens and decided to wait until morning to change them. The Hudson Bay Point blanket folded on the foot of the bed displayed a large amount of orange cat hair, "Been making yourself at home when I'm not looking, have you?" North swept as much of the hair off the blanket as he could with the palm of his hand.

Chores done and enough bourbon to relax him, North settled into the easy-chair. Only the light from the radio dial lit the room. He woke at the cat's meowing to go outside. He was pleasantly surprised that it was nearly a quarter past four in the morning. It meant that even if he didn't get back to sleep, he had enough to make it through the day. After relieving himself, he flopped onto the bed. The morning sun was just peeking through the bedroom window when he woke next.

Once shaved and dressed, North replaced the worn linens while the percolator did its job. Coffee under his belt and a quick glance through the cottage, and he was heading back to Howell.

At the Dunn-Wright, he wolfed down a plate of fried potatoes and eggs, and was his habit, wiped the plate clean with a piece of dry toast washed down with black coffee. North and Deweiss pulled into the Sheriff's Office parking lot at the same time. "You ready to head back to Brighton?" North called over the hood of his pickup.

Dennis Deweiss stared at North for a moment before he hunched over and put his hands on his knees. As North approached, he could see the deputy was sobbing. "What gives, Dennis?" North put his hand on Deweiss' shoulder.

Through the tears, Deweiss managed to say only one word, "Wilma."

"What happened?"

"S-She, uh," Deweiss blew his nose into his handkerchief, "she stopped breathing last night right after I fed her supper."

"Holy shit, Dennis," North was at a complete loss for words.

"Yeah, I know. I thought once she had the operation, she was going to be okay."

"So why are you here?"

"Where else should I be? My daughter and her husband are driving in from Escanaba in the Upper Peninsula. Shame the bridge isn't open yet," he said, referring to the Mackinaw Bridge, which was due to open in just a couple of weeks. "The ferry from St. Ignace to the Lower Peninsula only runs a couple of times a day at this time of year."

"Let's get you inside and find you some coffee," North pulled the backdoor to the station open. "Where's Wilma now?"

"Mr. Eberhart picked her up last night about nine."

Joyce walked into the building about the time that Deweiss had mentioned the mortuary, "Eberhart? What's going on?"

The deputy plopped into a chair. North spoke up, "His wife passed away last night."

"Wilma? No! I'm so sorry," Joyce dropped to her knees in front of Deweiss' chair and wrapped her arms around him. "You shouldn't be here," she scolded, "Let's get you home."

"No reason to be there." He looked at North, "Give me ten minutes to get my uniform on, and I'll be ready to go."

"You listen to me, Dennis," Joyce's voice was stern even as she fought back her own tears, "If you won't go home, then you'll stay here with me. Brick's a big boy; he can work on his own."

North lit a cigarette and picked a piece of loose tobacco off his lip. He put a hand on Deweiss' shoulder, "I'm good. You stay here with Joyce and wait for your daughter." He looked at Joyce, "I'll keep in touch. I'm heading to Pacek Sinclair in Brighton."

Chapter 11

North checked out the brown and white Dodge and made the drive down to Brighton. He spent most of his time contemplating the loss that Deweiss was feeling, knowing that there was no one he was that close to. Pacek Sinclair was on the south side of town and would have been the first service station a north-bound car would find along U.S. 23 in Livingston County.

The Dodge pushed air up the pneumatic tube, causing the bells inside the station to ring as the tires passed over it. North parked outside an open garage bay and stepped into the office area. A man about twenty years older than him sat in a chair behind the counter. Another man had just stepped out of the garage area and into the office. North gave him a once-over; early twenties, six-foot, barrel-chested, brown hair, thick neck with big hands. "I'm looking for a couple of cars that are missing," he looked at the older man, "Your name Pacek?"

"Yeah, Al Pacek. What's this about cars?"

"Two women have gone missing along with their cars," North was careful not to mention murder. "The Sheriff's Office is checking everywhere that those cars may be hidden. I see you have a storage lot behind the building; mind if I take a quick look?"

Pacek gave a shrug, "Whatever you're looking for, ain't here, but sure, take as much of a look as you'd like." Then to the youth, "Jimmie, why don't you take this deputy around back?"

The younger man visibly tensed. "What are you waiting for, you big galoot?" Pacek asked. Jimmie walked behind the counter and grabbed a ring of keys. North followed him with his eyes. It was then that he noticed that Pacek was missing his left leg from his knee down. Pacek spotted North looking, "Wasn't anything heroic if you're wondering. Lost it to gangrene cause of the diabetes."

Brick nodded and followed Jimmie out the front door and around the side of the garage. Two large galvanized steel gates hung from eight-by-eights. Jimmie fumbled with the padlock. "Problem with the lock there, Jimmie?"

"Nah, I just can't remember which key is which." On the third try, the old padlock popped open. Jimmie pulled one of the gates open a few feet and used his head to point for North to walk in.

"Why don't you go first, Jimmie? I'll follow you." The youth obliged, and North followed him into a storage yard of about forty-foot square. There were stacks of old tires and empty oil drums, wooden pallets, and general cast-offs. There was also a late thirties Ford coupe sitting on blocks and a cream-colored Ford F-100 pickup equipped with a tow harness.

North noticed mud along the sides of the pickup, "Have to tow someone from the mud, did you?" He saw Jimmie tense up again and changed his questions, "So you and Mr. Pacek related?"

Jimmie relaxed somewhat, "Yeah, he's my uncle. My pa was killed in the War, and my ma left when I was a kid. So my uncle took me in."

"Wow, that's rough. Do you live with your uncle?"

"Nah, he lets me sleep here. I got a bed in the back and a hotplate, and it works out. I also keep an eye on the place at night."

North lit a Pall Mall, "So, you're here by yourself a lot, I bet."

"Yeah, my Aunt Frances picks Uncle Al up around three, and I close up."

"What time do you close?"

"Usually around five or so. Depends. This time of year, sometimes earlier, cause it gets dark. In the summer, I usually stay open until six."

North tried to keep his voice even, but his experience was shouting that this guy looked right for the murders, and he matched the mortician's description of the kid who asked odd questions. North wanted to get a look at the truck's tires; he was confident that one of them would have a familiar cut across the tread. Jimmie locked the padlock and ran to gas up a DeSoto that had just driven over the cords. North walked back into the office.

Pacek looked up from the ledger he was working on, "Find what you were looking for there, deputy?"

With a shake of the head and a doff of the Bradmore, North smiled, "No, Mr. Pacek. I appreciate your cooperation." He looked out the window toward the pumps, "What can you tell me about your nephew?"

Pacek shook his head, "There's someone who just ain't going to go nowhere in life. No ambition and he's too dumb to pour piss outta a boot even if the directions were written on the sole."

About that time, Jimmie came in and put a dollar in the till. North made his way to the door before turning back as if an afterthought, "Jimmie tells me that he sleeps here at night."

"Ain't no law against that."

"No, sir. No law says he can't." North thought quickly, "But county health regulations say that the space must be safe and heated. Mind if I take a quick look. You know, in case I'm ever asked about it."

"Hell, check the ladies' room if you want. I don't care." Pacek looked at his nephew, "Step aside, Jimmie, let the man take a look so he can get on his way."

Jimmie stepped out of North's way, allowing him to walk into the storage room. A single light bulb with a metal shade hung from the ceiling in the middle of the room. In one corner was a card-table and folding chair. In the other corner was a metal-framed twin bed with a green wool army blanket and a pillow. There were no sheets on the bed, but North took note of the off-white pillowcase.

"So, Jimmie," North said as casually as he could, "this looks comfortable." Then, as he turned to leave, "By the way, are you also a Pacek?"

"Nah, ma was a Pacek, I'm a Nelson."

North stepped out the front door, "Well, thank you all for your cooperation." He drove to the IGA store and dialed 'O' on the payphone, located next to the mechanical horse. He asked the operator to connect him to the Sheriff's Office.

"Joyce, it's Brick. Get me the Sheriff."

"What's up?"

"I'll tell you right after I tell Sheriff Drake."

"And I thought we were friends," Joyce said with a small laugh.

There were two clicks as the call was transferred, the first as Joyce pulled the jack from her line, disconnecting herself, and the second as the jack was pushed into the Sheriff's line, "Drake."

"Tom, I think I may have found our murderer."

"You find the cars?"

"No, but I've got a young man who matches the description of the kid who asked Eberhart about how long it takes for a body to decay. He's got a bed at the service station and lives on-site, and get this, he's missing his bedsheets."

North heard Drake's lighter snap shut, "Pretty circumstantial."

"There's a pickup there. I want to get a look at the tires; I'm willing to bet that one of them has a cut across it. But it's behind a locked gate. I'm going to need a search warrant if I want to take a look at it."

Drake took a pull on his cigarette, "Small problem. Judge Williamson left this morning for Ann Arbor."

"Well, let's find him! I need to check those tires."

"It's homecoming weekend; tens of thousands of partiers are descending on Ann Arbor. We're not going to find the Judge. It'll have to wait until Monday."

"Bullshit!"

"Take a breath there, Brick. Use your head. There's got to be another way to check out that truck."

North lit his own cigarette. "We could have Joyce call and say her car is broken down and she needs a tow. Have him go to some address where I can take a look at the tires."

"And if you find the damaged tire, any good lawyer would claim entrapment. No, we've got to do this smart. If he's our guy, we need to have a rock-solid case against him." The phone was quiet for a few moments, "Brick, are you still there?"

"Yeah, I'm here. Just got an idea. I'm going to head back and trade out this official car with my pickup. I'll come back down here and stake out the station. If he goes anywhere, I'll follow him and see if I can't get a look at those tires. In the meantime, would you mind having Joyce check to see if there's any record for a James Nelson? Probably in his early twenties."

Drake made a note, "Gotcha. Check in with me when you exchange cars."

"Yes, sir." North put the handset back onto the cradle. Twenty minutes later, he was back in Howell.

"Brick," Joyce called out as he stepped into the office, "The Sheriff had me lookup records on a James Nelson."

North propped himself on the corner of her desk, "Yeah. Did you come up with anything?"

She picked up a folder and handed it to North, "Got a little something on one James Lloyd Nelson, born in Brighton, May seventeenth, thirty-five."

"That's got to be our guy." North flipped through the pages, "Been in a few fights. Wow, the idiot spent his twenty-first birthday in a holding cell here for drunk and disorderly." North lit a cigarette, "I guess that's one way to celebrate."

Joyce chuckled, "We don't get the best and the brightest in these parts."

"His uncle said he wouldn't be able to pour piss out of a boot."

"He did not!"

"Yes, he did. So, big, dumb, and with an angry streak. Sound like someone capable of rape and murder?"

Leaning forward, Joyce put her hand on his forearm and gave it a little squeeze, "Do me a favor?"

North looked at the hand on his arm, then at the receptionist, "What's that?"

"Be careful. This guy sounds like trouble."

"Thanks, doll. I'll do that." North crushed the Bradmore onto his head and strolled through the building's back door into the parking lot. He folded his suit jacket and put it on the passenger seat. The tie was put onto the coat, and he pulled the red and black Mackinaw from under the rear window and slipped it on. With the collar pulled up, he looked like just another farmer in a green pickup. It was a three cigarette drive back to Pacek's service station.

Across U.S. 23 from the station was a farm co-op; his pickup blended into the scenery. He parked facing Pacek's and waited. Over an hour, a few cars had stopped in for gas. Nelson had jogged out to meet each car, pumped gas, checked under the hood, and made change. But the pickup remained locked out of sight behind the towering galvanized gates.

Chapter 12

John Allison charged into the sumptuous outer office of Oftermatt Real Estate. Framed black and white photos of homes for sale in the LaSalle Harbor area hung on the walls. An attractive blonde sat behind a modern desk, the type with no drawers underneath, which perfectly framed her long legs. "Good afternoon, sir. How may I assist you?" she said as Allison walked past her toward a closed office door. "Sir! You can't go in there!"

"I'll go wherever the hell I want!" he spat. Allison flung the office door open, startling the regular occupant along with a couple who seemed to be signing a contract. "Out! Get the hell out of here!" He shouted at the couple.

The distinguished-looking man, who had been seconds before seated behind the desk, jumped to his feet, "Get out of here, John. I'll call you later." Then to the couple, "Excuse the interruption. Just a misunderstanding."

"No misunderstanding!" The mayor looked at the clients, "Get out of here and leave us alone. We have some personal business to discuss." the couple quickly left.

"John, I don't know what you think you're doing…"

"I'm looking for justice for my daughter."

"Am I supposed to know what you're talking about?! Get the hell out of my office before I call the police!"

Allison turned and locked the office door, "Your son beat and raped my daughter. Don't pretend you don't know anything about it."

"Bobby wouldn't…"

"Bullshit. You and I pressured the DA last year to get him off the hook. That's not going to happen again."

Oftermatt looked around the room, trying to come up with an answer, "That girl's parents didn't want to press charges."

"How much did that cost you? But that still didn't get him off the hook, did it? She was thirteen, and it was statutory. That's why we had to pressure the DA. And now he's done it again. This time it's my daughter, and this time he's going to pay."

"What'll it take to settle this, like gentlemen?"

Allison pulled a handgun from his waistband and pointed it toward Oftermatt's head, "There are no gentlemen in this room, Will. There's only a lying bastard and me. I might have been a gentleman before you pulled me down to your level with promises of power."

"John, don't be stupid!"

"Too late for that! I was stupid the moment that I thought following you would benefit me."

In the outer office, the blonde heard most of the conversation between her boss and the mayor, followed by two gunshots.

Chapter 13

After almost two hours of watching Pacek's Sinclair, North considered calling the station to ask for a tow. He recalled Drake's comments and knew that any evidence he gained through deception would be thrown out of court. He looked at the Bulova on his wrist. It was a little past two o'clock. Sylvia would be at the train station in less than two hours.

Another thirty minutes passed, North kept his mind occupied by counting the cars that drove past on the two-lane highway. He was just about to go into the co-op seeking a toilet when he saw Jimmy walk out of the station and open the metal gates. Minutes passed before the cream-colored Ford pulled out. Jimmy jumped out of it, closed the fence, and put the padlock back in place. North turned the key and pressed the starter button. Nelson pulled out onto U.S. 23, heading toward downtown Brighton. North followed at a safe distance. Nelson stopped at the Post Office and walked inside.

Knowing that whatever Jimmy was doing inside would take only moments, North jumped out of the Dodge and began looking at the tires of Pacek's truck. With one eye on the Post Office's steps and the other on the tires, he made a quick trip around the F100. He was almost sure there was a cut on the passenger side rear tire, but as luck would have it, the slice in the tread was on the bottom of the tire. Without standing on his head, there was no way to be sure. He reached into the bed of the truck and pulled out a hand of leaves that looked like the Dogwood leaves that Deweiss had pointed out earlier in the week. His gut told him everything he needed to know, but he'd still have to get to the tire.

Nelson came down the concrete steps of the Post Office just as North walked away from the truck. With the Mac's collar pulled up and the brim of his hat down, he was convinced he hadn't been recognized. He sat in the Dodge for a few minutes after Nelson pulled away. There would be another time to see that tire, but now he needed to get to Ann Arbor and pick up Syl.

Traffic in the city on the Friday afternoon of homecoming weekend was the busiest North had encountered in many years. He finally found a parking space and had just gotten his jacket and tie on as the train was announced. He stood on the platform, looking up and down the train cars trying to catch sight of Sylvia. It seemed like hundreds of riders, all wearing the maize and blue of the University of Michigan, were trying to push out at the same time. She came out of the second car behind the revelers. North chuckled; her green suitcase seemed larger than she.

"Brick!" she shouted. Dropping the suitcase and her cosmetic bag, she ran into his arms. He bent down and kissed her. She threw her arms around his neck and lifted her feet off the platform, "It's been a month since I've seen you, but it feels like years."

"It's good to see you too, doll. Is that all the luggage you've got?" He asked sarcastically.

Sylvia gave him a teasing stare, "What? You think I need more?"

He laughed and pushed into the sea of maize and blue to grab her bags. North carried the suitcase in his left hand and held her close with his right. She nestled in under his arm and held onto her purse and cosmetic bag as they made their way through the depot and out onto the street.

"It's so cold," she said as they stepped out into the street.

"The truck'll be warm, and I'll get a fire going in the cottage the minute we get in." Three minutes later, they were at the pickup. He held the passenger door open, and she slid onto the bench seat where she took up residence in the middle of the cab. He placed her bags in the bed of the pickup before getting in. The Dodge fired up, and as promised, heat began blowing in. "Have you eaten anything? Do you want to grab a bite?"

"No and no. I'm not really hungry. Guess I'm too excited to be with you."

He reached past her knees and pushed the gearshift into first. With a lurch, they headed toward Hell. The pickup had just pulled onto Miller Avenue when North saw his date for the evening step out of a beauty salon, her dark hair done up in a French Twist. "Gwen!" North exclaimed.

"Gwen? What?"

North recovered, "When. When did you get on the train?"

She gave him a curious look, "About eleven, why?"

"Just curious."

Sylvia put her head on North's shoulder as he followed the backroads. Forty minutes after leaving the depot, he pulled up next to the cottage. Realizing that she'd fallen asleep, he gently woke her, "Hey, doll. We're home."

She blinked the sleep out of her eyes and looked at the small faded white clapboard cottage with peeling green trim. "So, you spent your childhood here?

"Weekends and vacations mostly." He walked her to the front door, where they were met by the marmalade cat.

"Is this the roommate you mentioned?" Sylvia giggled.

"Ha, him? I'm his meal ticket. That's all."

Sylvia bent down and scratched the cat's head. "He's cute. What do you call him?" she said over the cat's purrs.

"Gatto."

"Gatto?"

"It's Italian for cat," North said as he opened the door.

"You called your cat, 'Cat'?"

North turned on the light, "He's not my cat."

The cat began doing figure-eights around North's legs. "Tell that to him," Sylvia said with a laugh.

North pointed out the two doors on the wall opposite the entrance, "The room on the left is the bedroom, the other is the bath."

Sylvia took in the cottage with its mismatched furniture, dusty Venetian blinds, and old rag rugs. It was then that she spotted the flowers, set in a coffee can, on the table, "Are those for me?"

"Hope you like them."

"You've never bought me flowers before!" She turned and gave him a kiss.

"I figured they would brighten this dump up." He lit a cigarette before turning his attention to the stove, "Let me get a fire going and then I'll go out and grab your bags. You want a drink?"

"I need something; I just can't get warm," she pulled the lapels of her coat up under her chin. North grabbed a chair from the kitchen table and placed it near the small stove. It wasn't long before a fire was casting warmth throughout the main room of the cottage. Her suitcase was placed in the bedroom and her cosmetic bag on his old dresser, which occupied a bathroom wall. He turned up the small electric heater, which he used to keep the pipes from freezing. Its coiled wire heating element glowed red in the darkness of the bathroom.

While Sylvia poured a drink for each of them, North brought in wood from the pile that had been delivered next to the cottage. He stacked the wood next to the stove and grabbed his drink. He moved her to the sofa. "You feel like you're warming up," he said as she rested against his chest.

"I'm still freezing," she said as she took a sip of the bourbon in her glass.

North pulled her closer, "Then, let me warm you some more." They sat on the sofa until she fell asleep again. He sipped at his bourbon, finally slipping out from under her when Gatto began to demand his dinner. He fed the cat, opened a tin of beef stew, and dumped it into a saucepan. Taking the loaf of bread from the cabinet, he sliced a couple of thick pieces, these he put on the flat top of the cast iron stove to toast. When the meal was warm, he woke Sylvia, "Hey doll, I've got some supper for you."

She yawned, "Hmmm? Oh, I'm sorry. All I've done is sleep since you picked me up."

Jokingly he said, "You should have slept on the train."

"I did. I must have a cold or something. Sorry to ruin your plans."

He smiled and ran his fingers through her hair, "The only plans I have are to be with you, and here you are."

She got up and walked to the table. North placed the stew and toast onto the table and sat down. Sylvia stirred the stew around with her spoon for a while but didn't eat any. "I know it's not Mammina's," he said, referring to a favorite restaurant back in LaSalle Harbor.

"Oh, the food is good. My throat is sore, and I've got a headache. I didn't sleep well last night. I'm probably just tired from that and the excitement of the trip."

"I've got some aspirin, and I bought some of that Lipton tea you like. You want either of those?"

"Do you have milk for the tea?"

He rose, leaned over, and kissed her on the head before speaking, "I've got that covered."

Sylvia put on a slight smile, "Then, yes. I'll have tea and a couple of those aspirins. If you don't mind, could you take the stew? I'll keep the toast, though."

"Sure thing, doll. You know I'm not much of a nursemaid, but I'll do my best."

"I'll be better in the morning, and you can show me around Hell. How many levels have you gotten to so far?" she asked, referring to Dante's Inferno. He gave her a quizzical look. She chided, "Where did you go to school? Didn't they teach the classics?"

"I just might have forgotten. What levels? I thought there was Hell, and that was it."

"There's lust, greed, gluttony, anger, violence, and a couple more."

"That sounds like just another day on the job."

She laughed softly, "Ouch, laughing just makes my head worse. So you haven't told me much about this job of yours." While water for the tea boiled, North gave her a rundown of what had transpired. "So, you're a deputy sheriff now?"

"Well, I'm really just helping the Sheriff out. He deputized me to make it official. It's not like I'm getting paid."

Sylvia sipped her tea and nibbled on the toast, "My mom always gave me tea and toast when I wasn't feeling well."

North laughed, "I hope you aren't thinking of me in a maternal way."

"Not a chance, not even here in Hell." She gave an involuntary shiver.

"You still cold?"

"I am," she wrapped her arms around herself.

"The water-heater works pretty good. You want to take a hot bath before we crawl into bed?"

"Not by myself."

North smiled and went to fill the tub.

Chapter 14

Doc Howard pushed the doors from the surgical theatre open and walked into the waiting room. The front of his white gown was covered in blood. He peeled off the rubber gloves as he approached Tiffin, who was asleep in a green vinyl chair, "Barry?" Howard whispered. Tiffin reflexively jumped.

Rubbing the sleep from his eyes, the detective gave a yawn before answering, "How'd he do?"

The doctor reached under the surgical gown and grabbed a package of cigarettes, "It was touch and go, but he'll live."

"When can I talk to him?"

"I don't have an answer for that. I'm going to have to keep him sedated for a while. Facial trauma like he has is amongst the most painful of injuries. I've had to remove the majority of the orbit under his right eye and cheekbone. The bullet traveled downward through the sphenoid sinus, through the roof of his mouth, and exited his left cheek, blowing out the first through third molars and connective tissue."

Barry reached for an offered cigarette, "Holy crap, Doc. What do you suppose happened?"

"Best guess would be that as he was pulling the trigger, he had second thoughts, and the gun went off as he was trying to lower it away from his head."

"So, murder and attempted suicide," Tiffin sucked the warm smoke into his lungs.

Doc Howard nodded, "The courts may find him not guilty on the one charge, but he'll be paying for the other for the rest of his life."

"Have you had a chance to examine Oftermatt yet?"

"His body is down in the morgue. I'll do an autopsy in the morning to make it official," the doctor took a drag on the cigarette. "But, the cause of death is pretty obvious. Allison's bullet entered through the left eye and exited out the back of the cranium. He would have been dead before he hit the floor."

"Can I get Allison's clothes and personal effects? I want to see if there's anything there that'll help me put all of this together."

Howard nodded and used his head to point to the door that he had most recently come through, "They're in the corner of the operating room. I'll get someone to bag them up for you."

A handful of reporters were waiting for Tiffin as he walked out of the hospital carrying a brown paper bag. One from the LaSalle Palladium, one from the Detroit Free Press, and the third from the South Bend Tribune. All three began calling questions as Tiffin tried to push past to get to the Mainline.

"Is it true that Mayor Allison killed Mr. Oftermatt?"

"Is Allison alive? Will he stand trial?"

"Mr. Oftermatt's secretary said that the mayor stormed into the office and was yelling about Oftermatt's son? What can you say about that?"

Tiffin pushed through them as one called out, "Would you care to make a statement?"

The detective stopped and turned back to the reporters, "Yes, I would."

All three of them raised their notepads, pencils hovered over blank pages.

Tiffin paused, choosing his words carefully before speaking, "Go to hell."

Chapter 15

The cottage's stove was as hot as it could get, and the space heater in the bathroom was dialed to the maximum setting. The two soaked in the old claw-footed tub until the water was just beginning to cool down. North sat behind Sylvia and held her; she rested her head against his chest. She felt tiny in his arms. "You stay here, and I'll run a little more hot water. Then I'll see what I can do to make the bed a little warmer," he said as he climbed over the wall of the tub.

Sylvia watched him dry himself off. His sinewy body showed the scars of the rugged roads he'd traveled. "Brick?"

"What's up, doll?"

"I'm sorry," she began to cry. "I've been dying to be with you, and now I'm ruining our weekend."

He wrapped the towel around his waist, "We're together, aren't we?"

"Yeah, but...," she began to say.

"It's okay. You'll feel better tomorrow, and I'll show you around Hell."

"Do me a favor?"

"Sure. What do you need?"

"Bring me a couple more aspirin. My head really hurts."

North left the bathroom, closing the door behind him. Damp and covered only in a towel, the chill in the main room took him by surprise. "Brrr," he said, only realizing after the sound came out that he'd made it aloud. He took the cast iron skillet and put it on the stove before grabbing the Bayer Aspirin bottle and filling a glass with water at the sink.

He gave her two aspirin and excused himself. He took the skillet and, walking into the bedroom, slid it under the covers at the foot of the bed. North then unfolded The Hudson Bay blanket, which he hadn't needed, and put it over the old double bed. He picked up his wristwatch; it was only eight o'clock.

Walking back into the main room, he rapped on the bathroom door frame, "You pruney enough yet?" he joked as he opened the door.

"I don't feel very pretty, that's for sure."

North looked over the blonde in the bathtub, "You look gorgeous to me."

She giggled, "You're only saying that because I'm naked in your bathtub."

"Well, there is that."

"Brick!" she called out, perhaps only half teasingly.

"Let's get you out of the water, and you can be mad at me later." She grabbed his offered hand. North was surprised at how much of a challenge it was for her to pull herself up. He gently drew her out of the tub, "You feeling okay, doll?"

"To be honest," she said as he began to dry her off, "I don't know. I'm exhausted, and my neck and head are really killing me."

"Let's get you dry, and we'll get you into bed." He gently rubbed her down with the towel, lingering perhaps a little longer over some places than others. He had always considered himself a loner, but Sylvia's telegram earlier in the week had caused him to realize how much he'd missed her company.

She hadn't planned on wearing the flannel pajamas that she'd packed until she'd gotten to her parent's home in the Virginia Park neighborhood of Detroit. But they were welcome along with a pair of heavy socks she'd brought for hiking. North helped her get dressed and held her for a moment, "You're still only wearing a towel!" she said when she was finally covered from neck to toe.

He looked down and laughed, "You may be cold, but I'm not." North reached under the covers and pulled the skillet out.

"You had a pan in the bed?!"

"I warmed it up; learned it from my mother. I think you'll appreciate that when you climb in." He held the covers for her as she slipped under the covers.

"Oh! That's nice," she sighed.

"Told you," he said as he pulled the covers over her. "I'll be back in a moment." North found Gatto sleeping in the kitchen near the stove and pushed him out the front door before turning out the lights. Clouds filled the night sky, blocking out the little light the waning crescent of the moon would have offered. Darkness took on a new meaning when there were no lights for miles in any direction. He made his way into the bedroom and dropped the towel before slipping next to the now sleeping Sylvia. He spooned in behind her; she was almost too warm to hold.

North rose every couple of hours and fed the stove. On his second trip up, he pulled on a pair of boxers and an undershirt. Whatever expectations he'd had for this night had long since evaporated. He'd been unable to fall asleep but was glad that Sylvia was sleeping soundly. He turned on the small lamp next to the sofa, grabbed the Old Quaker and a deck of cards. It was going to be a long night.

"Brick?" The voice came from what seemed like a thousand miles away. "Brick, where are you?" He jerked himself awake; the remains of a game of solitaire were splayed across the kitchen table. He hadn't realized that he'd fallen asleep.

"I'm here, doll." He pushed himself up and walked into the dark bedroom.

"I must have had a fever that broke; I'm really wet," Sylvia sounded tired.

"I'm too much of a gentleman to say anything about that," he turned on the lamp next to the bed.

"Yeah, but you just did." North was glad to see her smile. "Do you have any dry PJs I can change into?" she asked.

"I don't know if you've noticed, but I'm not exactly a pajama kind of guy. Let me see what I can find for you." North opened the wardrobe and pulled out a flannel shirt, "Don't suppose this would work."

Sylvia gave the green and blue shirt a once over, "You never struck me as a plaid kind of guy."

He smiled as he carried the shirt over to her, "Oh, you'd be surprised. I've split enough wood since I've been up here that I'm beginning to think I should have been a lumberjack."

She pulled her pajama top over her head and held out her hand for the shirt. North couldn't help but stare. She really was beautiful. "You going to give me that shirt, or are you going to make me beg?"

"Let me think about that for a moment." Sylvia gave a teasing glare, North handed her the shirt. "I'm glad you're feeling better."

"I'm drained, and my neck and head are still killing me, but at least the fever's gone, " she buttoned the flannel shirt and took off her pajama bottoms. Sylvia looked around the room, "Where's Gatto?"

"Gatto? I kicked him out hours ago. He never spends the night. Why? You become attached to him or something?"

She smiled, "I'm just glad that you made a friend. Now, if you'll excuse me, I need to use the little girls' room," she began to walk around North, who was standing at the foot of the bed but stumbled drunkenly over her own feet.

North reached out and grabbed her before she fell, "You okay, doll?"

"I guess that fever really wiped me out. I'm okay." He released his grip from around her waist and walked next to her to the bathroom. "I'm a big girl. I can go by myself." After a drink of water, she was back in bed. North followed as soon as he loaded the stove's firebox.

The sun was just creeping over the horizon when North was awakened to a pounding on the door. He rolled out of bed and grabbed the .38 from the nightstand. Flipping the cylinder open, he checked that all six rounds were there before quietly closing it. He crossed the living room, avoiding the view of the three small windows set in a diagonal across the door. He pulled the door open and thrust the revolver into the face of a young man on the other side. It was the deputy he'd met earlier in the week at Whitmore Lake. "Majors, right?" North said as he looked through the sights on the .38 and into the eyes of the deputy on his porch. He lowered his gun.

The deputy swallowed hard, "Uh, yeah. Sheriff Drake asked me to have you come to the office."

"Tell Sheriff Drake I wasn't home."

"I can't lie to the Sheriff, sir," the voice of the young deputy was shaking.

"Then tell him that I said to go to hell. And stop calling me sir."

"I can't tell him that either," the voice was beginning to sound desperate.

"Oh fuck it," North whispered as he fully opened the door. "Come in but be quiet. Someone's asleep in the other room."

Majors lowered his voice, "I'm sorry, but the sheriff said it's important, and you need to come."

"Well, it damn well better be important. Go ahead and head back. I need to get dressed. I'll be there as soon as I can." Majors nodded, squared his campaign hat on his head, and walked out.

North took some clothes into the bathroom and dressed. He pulled on his worn leather shoulder holster and slipped the Colt under his arm. "Hey, Syl," he whispered into her ear.

"Hmmm?" she replied through closed eyes.

"I've got to run into town. Something came up, and the sheriff wants to see me."

"Mhmm."

"I've got the stove nice and hot, and there's plenty of wood next to it. I'll be back as quickly as I can. We'll go see the sights when I get back." He leaned down and kissed her on the side of her head, "I love you."

"Mhmm," she mumbled.

North grabbed the Mac, pushed the Bradmore onto his head, and locked the front door behind himself. He smiled, thinking about the petite blonde, warm and snug in his bed.

His first stop in Howell was at the Dunn-Wright, where he got the thermos filled with fresh coffee. He walked into the backdoor of the Sheriff's Office just forty minutes from the time Majors had left the cottage.

"Brick," Drake shouted from his office. "Thanks for coming in."

"I didn't think I had a choice. What's going on?"

The Sheriff pulled a cigarette out of the box on his desk, "We've got two missing girls. According to their parents, they were going to Ann Arbor to take in some of the homecoming festivities."

Lighting a Pall Mall, North sat across from the sheriff, "Who are they?"

"Brenda Miller, nineteen, and Kimberly Johnson, eighteen."

"When were they last seen?" North picked a piece of tobacco off his lip and rolled it between his fingers.

Drake took a pull on his cigarette, "The Miller girl picked up the other at approximately half-past four. They were going to meet some high school friends who attend the University."

"Who reported them missing?"

"Their parents. Apparently, the Millers and Johnsons have been phoning each other every hour or so, starting when the girls didn't come home at midnight as planned. Mr. Miller called at six this morning."

North pulled out his notepad, "Where's the Miller house?"

"Four seventeen West Crane just off of Gregory. You planning on going there?" Drake flicked the inch of ash off the end of his cigarette.

"Gotta start somewhere. You suppose Majors is available to go with me?"

Drake picked up the phone and pressed one of the four buttons along the bottom edge, "Joyce, where's Majors?" He paused while the receptionist responded, "Okay. When he gets back here, North needs him." He replaced the receiver on the cradle and looked at North, "Majors is gassing up the car. He should be back here in ten minutes or so."

North nodded and walked to the desk he'd been using. He placed his cigarette in the ashtray and transferred some notes from his pad into the file he had started on Jimmy Nelson. He had just finished his second thermos lid of coffee when the young deputy entered the building. "Majors! You up to accompany me to talk with the missing girls' parents?"

The deputy smiled, "Yeah! That'd be great. Just got to let the Sheriff know."

"Already done. Let's get going." North stood, crushed the worn fedora onto his head, and called up to Joyce, "Majors and I are heading over to the Miller house on West Crane."

"Got it," she shot back.

"You wanna drive?" Majors asked as they got to the Dodge.

"No, you know the town better than me. You drive."

"What's the address?" Majors asked as he pushed the gearshift into first.

"Four seventeen West Crane." The address was less than five minutes from the Sheriff's Office. The house, a bungalow, was neat, and the yard tidy. A few cars occupied the curb in front. Majors parked on the opposite side of the street, facing the wrong direction. Loud voices could be heard coming through the open door at the Millers.

"I didn't think it was a good idea for the girls to be traipsing off to Ann Arbor," North heard a woman say as he and Majors climbed the porch steps. "If you hadn't given permission to your Brenda, Kimmie wouldn't have pressured us to go."

Another woman countered, "Don't go blaming this on Brenda! We both know your Kimberly isn't an angel!"

"How dare you?!" Mrs. Johnson's voice went up an octave. "Like Brenda is…"

North noticed that the husbands were standing back, not entering the fray. He interrupted the pair of feuding middle-aged women, "Ladies, I'm Rick North from the Sheriff's Office, and this is Deputy Majors. May we come in?" Both of the women nodded, looked down, and separated as North and Majors entered the room.

North opened his notepad, "Okay, who's who?"

"I'm Stan, and that's my wife, Jane," a balding, middle-aged man said. "Brenda is our daughter."

North looked up from his notepad, "So, you're the Millers, is that right?"

"Yes," Mrs. Miller jumped in. "What are you doing to find our daughter?"

"Asking you questions to figure out where to start." North turned his attention to the other couple, "You're the Johnsons?"

Mrs. Johnson spoke up, "Yes, I'm Mary, and that's my husband, Bill."

"When did you last see your daughters?"

Mrs. Miller started to speak, but her husband cut her off, "Brenda left here about a quarter past four."

"Do you know what she was wearing?"

Mr. Miller turned to his wife, who gave him a look of exasperation. The missus answered North's question, "A navy blue skirt of heavy wool with a wide black elastic belt, a white cotton blouse, and a blue sweater."

"How about your daughter, Mrs. Johnson?"

"Kimmie was wearing a pink fuzzy Angola rabbit hair sweater with a white dickie under it. Her skirt is pink and white stripes. The stripes go back and forth, not up and down."

"What time did Miss Miller arrive at your house?"

"Close to half-past four."

"Did they leave right away?"

"Brenda came in for a couple of minutes. She was in a hurry. Said she needed to gas up the car before they left town."

North looked to the Millers', "What kind of car was Brenda driving?"

Mrs. Miller glared at her husband, "Tell him, Stan. You know better than I do."

"An Empire Red nineteen-fifty Chevy Styleline two-door."

North jotted down the details along with the license plate number, which Miller provided, "Who were they going to visit in Ann Arbor?"

"Joan Royston and Dee Gagnier," Mrs. Johnson answered. "The girls went to high school together."

"Do you know where they were going to meet?"

The two sets of parents looked at each other. Bill Johnson finally tackled the question, "No idea, actually."

"One final question," North lit a cigarette, "do you have any photos of your daughters?"

Chapter 16

Armed with the Miller girl's graduation picture and a snapshot of Kimberly Johnson, North and Deputy Majors climbed into the car. "Where to?" Majors asked as he pressed the starter button.

"Pacek Sinclair in Brighton. But first, let's stop at the office and catch the Sheriff up before we go."

Twenty-five minutes later, they pulled over the pneumatic hose in front of the service station. North got out of the car and crushed his cigarette under his shoe, "Notice anything unusual?"

"No. What?" the deputy squared his hat. "What am I missing?"

North pointed to the business hours sign on the door, "It's after nine; they should be open."

"You think they overslept?"

"I don't know. Let's find out." North pounded on the door, "Nelson! Sheriff's officers, open up!" There was no answer. North pounded on the door harder, "Sheriff, open the door." Again, the command went unanswered.

Majors looked at North, "What do we do now?"

North nodded toward the tall galvanized gates that blocked the back of the garage, "Pull the car parallel to those gates." Majors did as he was instructed. North walked over and climbed onto the hood of the Dodge before looking over the gates. He jumped down and shouted at the deputy, "pull back and get me the tire iron from the trunk. I think it's safe to say that we have probable cause to have a look around."

Majors put the gearshift into reverse and slowly let the clutch out. The car rolled back about ten feet. He unlocked the trunk and dug behind the spare tire. Pulling the iron free, he handed it to North, "What do you mean 'probable cause?'"

"Kid, if you're going to be a deputy, you need to keep up on the law." North lodged the pointed end of the steel tool into the shackle of the Yale padlock. "The Supreme Court decided in Brinegar versus the United States," he paused to grunt as he pulled the padlock from its hasp, "that if we believe that a crime has been committed and a judge would probably issue a warrant, we get to go in." North pulled the gate open.

"But what crime has been committed?"

North pointed to the red 1950 Ford Styleline, "What was the license plate number Miller gave us?"

Majors looked at his notes, "YL 1207."

"And what's the plate number on the Ford over there?"

"YL...," the deputy looked at Brick, "That's the car!"

North walked up and opened the driver's door on the Chevy. He stooped in and came out holding a brown leather purse. He turned the contents out onto the trunk lid, picked up a wallet, and extracted an operator's permit, "Miller, Jennifer R." He pushed the contents back into the purse.

North brushed past Majors and walked briskly to the office door. One kick and the door burst open. "Nelson!" he yelled as he walked into the storage room. There was no one there. He flipped the light switch next to the door and took a look around. An army blanket was on the floor, as were a pair of panties. A torn white dickie and another purse were behind the storage room door. The hotplate that had once sat on a folding table was also on the floor, its fabric-covered electrical cord torn off. "Shit!" North exclaimed as he walked to the front counter, picked up the phone, and dialed zero.

"Operator."

"Get me the Sheriff's Office."

A familiar, gruff female voice answered, "Livingston County Sheriff's Office."

"Joyce, it's North."

"Brick! Find anything?"

"Yeah. Get me an address for an Al Pacek, probably here in Brighton."

"Do you want me to call you back?"

"No, I'll hold," he lit a cigarette and offered the pack to Majors.

The deputy put his hand up, "I don't smoke."

North shrugged and put the pack back into his pocket. A few minutes passed before Joyce returned to the line, "I found an Alvin Pacek at 611 Washington Street."

"That's got to be our guy," he crushed out the cigarette in the melamine ashtray on the counter, "Thanks, doll."

They secured the station as best they could and drove into the older part of town. Within a few minutes, they were knocking at the door of the Pacek house. A middle-aged woman answered it, "May I help you?"

"I'm Deputy North; this is Deputy Majors. We need to speak with Al Pacek."

She turned toward the kitchen, "Al, the police are here to talk to you."

"What the hell?!" Pacek came rolling out from the back of the house using his one foot to propel the wheelchair forward. He looked at North, "You again? What do you want?"

"Where's your nephew?"

Pacek looked confused, "Jimmy? He's at the station."

"No, he isn't. Where would he go?"

"I don't know. Jimmy should be there; we open at nine."

"Today, he didn't."

"What's this about?" Mrs. Pacek looked between the deputies.

"We've got two missing girls, and their car was hidden in the yard behind your building."

Pacek got defensive, "Where do you think we park the cars we tow?"

North bent down toward the man in the wheelchair, "The car is in the back, but the girl's personal belongings were in the storage room."

"Maybe they left items in the car. Jimmy probably brought them inside for safe keeping."

"I doubt they left their underwear! Now, where the hell would he go?"

Mrs. Pacek turned to her husband, "I told you that boy was no good. Just like his father, always up to something he shouldn't be."

North put his hands on the arms of the wheelchair and looked directly into Pacek's eyes, "Where would he go?!"

"I-I don't know." The older man looked confused.

"The cottage," Mrs. Pacek blurted out, "He probably went to the cottage."

North turned toward her, "Where? Where's this cottage?"

"Over at Hi-Land Lake."

"Hi-Land Lake, in Hell?" North stood up and looked at her, "Where at Hi-Land Lake?"

"Oakridge Court, off of Weiman. We haven't been there since," she looked at her husband, "since Al lost his leg."

North looked at his partner, "John, use the phone and let the office know where we're going." Then to the Paceks, "You keep any weapons there? Maybe a rifle or shotgun?"

Al Pacek looked up, "No, just some fishing gear."

"If your nephew does show up here, I need you to call the Sheriff's Office right away." North stepped onto the porch.

Majors returned from the kitchen, "Okay. Done."

"Give me the keys. I know exactly where we're going." The deputy tossed the keys to North and climbed into the passenger door.

North dropped down U.S. 23 and picked up Michigan 36, which he took west. In less than twenty minutes, he was in Hell. He turned onto Weiman and worked his way down the rutted dirt road to Hickman Court and North's End. "I'm going to run in and use the head and check on my friend. Be out in a couple of minutes."

"Okay. Where's Oakridge Court?" Majors asked.

"Next road up on the right. But you hang tight here. I don't want to spook Nelson."

Majors nodded, "Okay."

As he slipped the key into the lock, North noticed the blinds were still closed. Stepping inside, he immediately felt the chill in the air. The fire in the stove had gone out hours before. "Syl?" There was no answer. "Sylvia!" he shouted as he ran to the bedroom. She was on the bed, not moving.

As he ran to the side of the bed, he noticed that Sylvia had vomited at some point after he had left. North put his hand on her shoulder to gently shake her; she was burning up. "Sylvia!" he shook her, "Syl! Wake up."

Her eyes opened; they were glassy. She looked through him.

"Syl, it's Brick. I need you to wake up, doll."

Sylvia's eyes widened. She used an arm to push him away as she mumbled something that North couldn't make out. What he could make out was that she seemed afraid. "It's okay, doll. It's me. I'm going to get you some help."

He wrapped the blanket around her, gently lifted her from the bed, and carried her outside. "Majors! Open the back door." The deputy jumped out of the car and opened the passenger side back door. Tenderly, he laid Sylvia on the backseat and climbed in, holding her. She looked around, wild-eyed. Again, she muttered something North couldn't understand.

"What's going on?" Majors asked.

"I don't know, but we need to get her to a hospital."

"What about Nelson?"

For just a heartbeat, North was torn between duty and his love for the woman he was holding. "Fuck Nelson. Where's the closest hospital?"

Majors put the car in gear and pulled away from North's End, "University of Michigan."

"You know the way?"

"Yeah, I can find it."

"Then go!" The Dodge sent gravel flying as it turned back onto Weiman. With each pothole Majors hit, Sylvia made a noise. When the car hit a large rut, Sylvia cried out. A single tear rolled down her cheek. At North's urging, Majors lit up the red lights on the car's roof and hit the siren. The few vehicles they encountered moved to the shoulder as they flew by. It seemed like they had driven hours before they arrived at the University. They crawled through the campus as thousands of people made the hike to the Stadium for the homecoming game. Majors tapped the siren a few times to encourage people to move out of the way. Finally, they were at the Emergency entrance to the hospital.

Chapter 17

Tiffin stopped by the Debois Bakery and grabbed a cheese danish on his way to the Safety Building. Once in the office, he shook a sizable amount of powdered coffee creamer into the black liquid in his cup. He stirred it with the communal spoon that sat on the table. Uher was at his desk, having beat Tiffin into the office by five minutes.

Chief Cummings was coming up the stairs just as Tiffin had sat down, "Don't get too comfortable. I just got the warrant allowing us to search both Allison's and Oftermatt's offices."

"I'm surprised you got a judge to issue that," Tiffin said as he took a bite from the danish.

Cummings smiled, "The note you found in Allison's pocket outlining what he and Oftermatt had done to keep Oftermatt's boy out of jail went a long way in helping the judge make the right decision."

Tiffin washed a bite of the danish down with coffee, "How do you want to proceed?"

The chief nodded toward Uher, "Dan and I will check out the major's office. There will be less grief with the City Council if I'm part of serving that warrant. You grab a uni," referring to a uniformed officer, "and serve the Oftermatt offices."

"I doubt if we'll find anyone there to open up for us," Tiffin finished the danish.

"Take a crowbar if you need to open the place up. These two used their influence to keep Oftermatt's son from being tried for statutory rape and to get North brought up on charges. I want both of those situations remedied." The chief looked at Uher, "You coming?"

Uher jumped to his feet and grabbed his hat, "Oh, yeah. I'm right behind you."

Tiffin picked up the phone on his desk. "Good morning, detective," a well-trained voice said, "how may I direct your call?"

"Morning, put me through to the Sergeant's desk."

"Yes, sir." There were a couple of clicks before the phone began to ring. "Sergeant Higdon."

"Ben, I need a uni to help me serve a warrant. Who have you got?"

"Well, good morning to you too, Barry. Let me see." There was a pause, "Will Brodeur just stepped out of the locker room. You want me to send him up?"

"No, keep him there. I'll be down in a minute." Tiffin depressed the switchhook and lifted it. Again he was connected to the switchboard. "Officer Brodeur and I are heading to the Oftermatt Real Estate Office."

"Thank you, detective."

Once on the main level of the Safety Building, Tiffin checked out the Ford Mainline. He smiled at Brodeur, who sat stiffly in the passenger seat, "Relax, Officer."

"I've never worked a search warrant before. And I know what Oftermatt did to Detective North."

Tiffin shook his head, "We don't know anything."

"The guys in the locker room…"

"The guys in the locker room don't know anything either. Scuttlebutt ends up having a life of its own. We need to do this search and keep our eyes open. Understood?"

"Yes, sir." Brodeur looked out the window for a minute, "Can I ask you a question?"

"Shoot," Tiffin said as he pulled in front of the real estate office.

"Is Detective North going to be able to come back?"

"I hope so, Will. I hope so."

Exiting the Ford, they noticed movement inside the office. Two men moved from the main room into the office in the back. Brodeur, following Tiffin's lead, pulled the gun from his holster. Tiffin pushed the door open and shouted, "Police! Put your hands up and step out here slowly."

The men, both wearing green coveralls, stepped into the front room of the office. Tiffin gave them the once over before directing them onto their knees. "Put your hands on your heads and don't move," he ordered. With a nod, Brodeur handcuffed the men while Tiffin kept his .38 trained on them. "Okay, who are you, and why are you here?"

The larger of the two men spoke, "We're here to clean the place up after what happened yesterday."

Tiffin gave each man a more serious going over. Their hair was trimmed and groomed. Their hands and nails showed no indication they labored for their wages. The overalls were new, and they were wearing well-maintained dress shoes. "Bullshit! What are you doing here?"

"I've said all we're going to say," the spokesman said with a bob of the head that indicated he was done speaking.

"We'll see if we can't loosen your tongue when we get you downtown." Tiffin looked at the other man, "What about you? You have anything to say?"

"No, I'm good."

"Brodeur, call for a paddywagon to collect these two while I see what they were up to."

While Brodeur made the call and kept watch over their captives, Tiffin took the time to look around. The first thing he noticed was the bloodstains on the carpet and the brain matter on the wallpaper behind where the want-to-be politician had stood. The second thing he noticed was the open safe in the corner of the room.

Inside the safe were contracts, deeds, and a small amount of cash. On the desk, Tiffin found what he suspected the men had come for. There, next to a canvas bag, was a checkbook, register, and a ledger book. He flipped through the ledger. In neat columns were dates, dollar amounts, and the reason for cash received or spent. One column listed the initials of some people; some were named. Among those named were some of the city, county, and state's most known officials, like Mayor John Allison. It seems payola was not below Mr. Oftermatt. One set of initials stuck in Tiffin's mind, "R.W., R.W? Why should I know who R.W. is?"

Brodeur looked up and shrugged, "Richard Wagner?" He emphasized the German pronunciation of the name.

"Who's Richard Vagner?"

Brodeur blushed, "Wrote German operas. Let me think." He paused for a few moments, "Robert Wilson."

"Okay, who's that?"

"One of the owners of the Detroit Lions."

"Well, at least you picked someone who's still alive this time. R.W.? It's not coming to me." Tiffin bundled up the evidence and cash, using the bag the would-be burglars provided. While they waited for the paddywagon, he went through Oftermatt's desk and file cabinets as well as the office secretary's. Nothing seemed out of the ordinary except for a manila envelope he found in the back of one of the drawers. It contained several compromising photos of men Tiffin recognized. Each man was in bed, and each was with the same woman, in the same room. Blackmail was apparently not below Mr. Oftermatt either.

Chapter 18

No one seemed to pay much attention to the Brown and White Dodge with Livingston County Sheriff's markings as it pulled under the University Hospital portico.

Majors looked over the seat to North, holding Sylvia, "Where should I park?"

"Just stop here and let me out." Brick slid Sylvia onto his lap, opened the door, and lifted her out of the car. He used his shoulder to push the door open and stood in the Emergency Room, "Can I get some help here?"

A young doctor in a starched white lab coat with a stethoscope draped over his neck turned at the sound of North's voice. Sylvia, wrapped in the old Hudson Bay Point blanket, lay limp in North's arms. "What's happened?"

"I found her an hour ago. She was agitated and didn't seem to recognize me. Now, I can't wake her, and she's got a high fever."

The doctor called an orderly to bring a gurney. North gently laid Sylvia on it. "What's her name?"

"Sylvia Kingston."

"Are you her husband?" the doctor asked as the gurney was rolled through a set of double doors into the innards of the hospital.

"No, I'm a friend."

"Well, Sylvia's friend. Go over to the counter there," he pointed with his head, "and the nurse will get her information."

North watched the doctor disappear through the doors where Sylvia had been taken moments before. He felt his throat tighten and a heaviness in his chest. His head spun from the sheer volume of thoughts that ran through it. Time took on an ethereal quality. "Sir?" a woman spoke from behind him. "Are you okay?" He realized that he had been staring at the tiled floor, how long he did not know. Turning, he looked toward the voice and recognized the owner.

Gwen Guinn seemed as surprised to see him as he was at seeing her, "Brick? What's going on?" Gwen was dressed all in white. A black stripe ran near the top of her white nursing cap.

"I just brought a friend in who seems very sick."

"Come over to the counter," Gwen's voice and cadence were very formal. "Let's get some information." She stepped behind the counter and sat down before rolling a form into the carriage of the typewriter, "What's your friend's name?"

"Sylvia Kingston."

"And her address?"

"She lives at the Sheffield Building on Pipestone Street in LaSalle Harbor."

Gwen tilted her head to the side, "What's she doing in Ann Arbor?"

Guilt was not something North experienced very often, but this was one of those occasions. He did not want to tell Gwen that she was there to visit him, "She was taking the train to her parent's house in Detroit, wasn't feeling well, and got off here."

"When was this?"

"Yesterday afternoon. I picked her up a little after four."

Nurse Guinn looked up into North's eyes, "Is this why you stood me up?"

"It is," North paused for a moment, "I'm terribly sorry."

"You don't need to apologize for helping a friend." She put her attention back onto the typewriter, "Do you have contact information for her family?"

"I don't. She may have an address book in her purse; I didn't think about grabbing it."

Gwen poised her fingers on the home keys of the typewriter, "How can we reach you if necessary?"

"You can leave a message for me at the Livingston County Sheriff's Office."

She began to type and stopped, "Is Brick your given name?"

"No. Richard, Richard North."

Gwen gave a reserved smile, "I think Brick fits you better."

North smiled back, "Any more questions?"

"Not right now."

He tipped his hat and walked back outside. It took him a few minutes to find the car and Majors. The young deputy was occupied watching a couple of co-eds sitting on a bench near the entrance. He sat up straight when North opened the door, "Is she going to be okay?"

"I wish I knew," North said as he put the Bradmore on the seat and pulled the pack of Pall Malls from the pocket of the Mac.

Majors waited while North lit the cigarette, "Where to?"

"Hi-Land Lake and make it quick."

Once clear of the crowded campus, Majors pushed the accelerator pedal down, and the big car sped out of town. In North's mind, the trip to Ann Arbor had taken forever. The return trip to Hell took less than thirty minutes. Majors eased the Dodge around the small lake, stopping the car on Weiman Road. At North's instruction, he parked the car across the narrow entrance to Oakridge Court, blocking the path to the main road.

"Let's walk from here," North said as he crushed the Bradmore onto his head and closed the car door very quietly.

Majors nodded his understanding, "Which cottage is theirs?"

"There are only a half-dozen cottages down here," North said, thinking of the midnight walks that he'd made down the lane. If he's here, it'll be the one with the cream-colored pickup."

They walked down the lane that was centered on a small peninsula that extended into the lake. Next to the second house on the left was Pacek's Ford. North put a finger to his lips and whispered to the young deputy, "Quietly go around to the back of the house. We don't want Nelson sneaking out the backdoor. Oh, and don't be seen."

Majors made his way around the house while North crept up on the pickup. He found exactly what he thought he'd find on the wooden floor of the bed of the truck; a body wrapped in an army blanket.

"Two girls missing, one body here," he thought to himself, "Where's the other girl?" His question was answered almost immediately by screams coming from the cottage.

"Please! Leave me alone. I promise I won't tell, just let me go!" the voice pleaded.

"Shut up! Just shut the fuck up. I gotta think." North recognized Jimmy Nelson's voice. He stooped and made his way to the front of the house. North tossed the Bradmore onto the ground and lifted his head to see into the window. Across the room was a petite brunette in a pink sweater. Tears had washed mascara down her cheeks. Her left cheek was bruised, and her eye was swollen.

"Just let me go. Please!"

"Shut up!" Nelson yelled. "Why did both of you have to be in the car? It's your fault, you know. If you hadn't been with her, you wouldn't be here."

North quietly climbed the three steps and onto the small porch. As Nelson continued to yell at the brunette, Brick planted his boot into the door just below the doorknob. As expected, the door frame splintered, sending shards of pine across the room. Nelson spun at the sound of the door crashing in and faced North's Colt. North knew he could easily make the shot just two yards away, but he could not be sure the bullet wouldn't pass through Nelson and into the girl. Nelson took the moment of hesitation to bolt through the house and out the back door. North fired one round that struck the edge of the door as Nelson ran past it.

"He's coming your way, Majors!" North yelled as he scrambled through the door that their suspect had just run through. Nelson, who had a good six inches and forty pounds on the young deputy, had used Majors as a tackling dummy. Majors was on his back, trying to regain his breath. Nelson had bolted into the bush behind the cottage and was nowhere to be seen. There was a smear of blood on Major's uniform where Nelson's shoulder had crashed into him.

North offered the deputy a hand up, "Looks like I hit him."

"I'm sorry I let him get past me," Majors tried to brush the blood off with his handkerchief.

"It happens, kid. Let's see how the girl is." They made their way back into the cottage.

The young woman was sobbing hysterically. "He killed Brenda!" she managed to choke out. "H-He raped her, and he killed her!"

North put on his softest voice, "Kimmie, right?"

"Yes."

"Did he hurt you, Kimmie?" North lowered himself and knelt in front of where she was seated.

For the first time since he had been in the house, she looked directly at North, "He hit me really hard." Then added, "With his fist."

"We're going to get you home to your mom and dad. Okay?"

Kimmie sniffed to clear her nose, "Okay."

"Can you tell me how you managed to meet this guy?" North pulled the Pall Malls from his pocket, Miss Johnson reached for one. North lit her cigarette, then his.

"Brenda needed gas, and this guy came out and started pumping the three dollars of gas that Brenda asked for," she took a drag on the cigarette and began to cough. "He cleaned the windshield and went to check the oil." Miss Johnson paused for a moment as if reliving the scene. "Then he told us that the fan belt was about to break, and Brenda said she didn't have extra money for any repairs." She paused.

Finally, North interrupted her thinking, "Then what happened?"

Coming out of her thoughts, Kimmie responded, "He said he'd fix it for free, and we could wait inside the office while he took care of it." North nodded his understanding. "Then Brenda saw that he wasn't working on the car; he was just standing in front of it. So she went out to tell him we were in a hurry." She paused to take another drag on the cigarette, "And he grabbed her and put a hand over her mouth and pulled her into the gas station and locked the door." Another long pause followed. Her attention was focused on the burning cigarette between her fingers.

Majors interrupted the silence, "What happened? Did he assault you?" North gave him a stern look and shook his head.

"I passed out when he hit me. Guess I hit my head on the counter. When I came to, he was on top of Brenda, and he had his hands around her throat." She paused for a moment and closed her eyes, "It was terrible. Then he got all agitated and wrapped her in a blanket. I was screaming. So, he stuffed an old rag in my mouth and then tied me up with a cord."

"Okay," North stood. "Majors, why don't you bring the car down here? You can take Miss Johnson back to town and get the Sheriff and Doc Von Boren back here."

"What're you going to do?"

"Stay here in case our boy shows back up."

Ten minutes later, with Kimberly Johnson in the back sear wrapped in a blanket from the trunk, Majors turned the car toward town. North went out to the pickup and checked for the key; it was not in the ignition. He lifted the hood and pulled the wire that ran between the coil and the distributor cap. This he put in his jacket pocket. He collected the Bradmore from under the front window and walked to the back of the cottage. He looked down the peninsula. Somewhere out there was a wounded man who had killed three times that North was aware of.

Clicking the lid of the Zippo lighter closed, North drew in a lung full of smoke. He spent some time going through the cottage as he tried to wrap his head around why Nelson would have dumped Monica Baker's body less than half a mile away from his family cottage. "Criminals aren't very bright," North mused to himself. "Why didn't he kill the Johnson girl?" He had no answer for that one.

He checked the time and figured he had at least half an hour before he could expect either the Sheriff or the Coroner. Brushing the dirt off the brim of the fedora, he pushed it over his mop of hair. The cylinder of the Colt dropped open at a touch of the release. North identified the round that he had fired and pulled the spent cartridge out with his fingernail. He reached into one pocket, then the others, trying to find the extra rounds he always carried with him. It was then that he realized he must have forgotten them in his haste to get out of the cottage earlier. "Damn!" he muttered. He returned the .38 to its holster before walking out the back door and toward the lake.

The lake was only twenty-five feet from the back of the cottage. North looked left and right. It made no sense for Nelson to run to the right; that path would have dead-ended at the tip of the peninsula. He decided to walk to the left, which would take him to Weiman Road. Nelson could be hiding in or around any of the closed cottages or, he could have walked to the main road and hitched a ride. One way or the other, Nelson was little more than an injured animal. Rational thought, even if he'd been capable of it before being shot, would undoubtedly have evaporated.

Chapter 19

LaSalle Harbor was not by any means a major metropolitan city. But, the combination of men coming in from the farms, sailors from the freighters, and truck drivers passing through, created a smorgasbord of problems. Gambling, prostitution, and drugs were commonplace, as was the occasional bar fight. For these and other issues, the police department maintained two paddywagons. One pulled in front of the Oftermatt Real Estate office within minutes of Brodeur's call.

The two coverall-clad men were assisted into the back and shackled to the parallel seats. A uniformed officer climbed into the back and shut the doors behind him. With a bang on the metal wall that separated the box the officer and prisoners were in from the cab, the converted Chevy panel van pulled away from the curb and headed toward the Safety Building.

Tiffin reached into his jacket pocket and pulled out a red seal which read, "These premises have been sealed by the LaSalle Harbor Police. All persons are forbidden to enter unless authorized by the LHPD." He signed his name to it and applied the seal to Oftermatt's inner office's frame and door. It would break should anyone open the door. He turned off the lights and applied another seal to the front door of the office. Brodeur gave a quizzical look, "The door's not locked. How's that seal going to keep someone from just walking in?"

"Because Will, my boy, locks only keep honest people honest."

Back at the Safety Building, Tiffin thanked Brodeur for his assistance, "He's all yours!" he shouted at the duty sergeant before heading up the stairs to the detective squad room. The coverall twins were shackled to a bench that was bolted to the floor outside the interrogation room. Tiffin sat down at his desk and began to make notes while waiting for Chief Cummings and Uher to return from the Mayor's Office. They arrived within twenty minutes of Tiffin's return.

"What've you got?" Tiffin's voice was full of excitement.

The chief looked at the pair shackled to the bench, "Oh, I think you win the who-goes-first contest."

Tiffin stood and nodded toward the pair, "These fine gents were going through Oftermatt's offices. Told me they were a cleaning crew. They'd gotten the safe open and were collecting items to remove." He touched the canvas bag on his desk, "I've got what they had found here along with some other, uh, material."

"Other material? Like what?"

Tiffin handed the chief the manila envelope. Cummings carefully slid the photos free and quickly flipped through them. "There are a few politicians who are praying we don't find these," he whispered

"That's pretty much what I thought," Cummings handed the envelope back. "Did you two come up with anything at the Mayor's office?"

Cummings took the pipe from his breast pocket, loaded the bowl, and struck a match before answering. "Resistance," he said as he coaxed the fire into the moist tobacco.

"But you had a warrant!"

"A couple of the Councilmen wanted us to know that information pertaining to city business was off-limits." Cummings took a gentle pull on the pipe.

Tiffin lowered his voice into a conspiratorial tone, "I don't suppose the Councilmen are among those we have compromising photos of?"

The chief nodded as he said, "I can't confirm that."

"So the answer is yes?"

Cummings nodded again, "I can't say."

Barry inclined his head in understanding, "Until we pull a case together?"

"Exactly. I'm beginning to think that many of those involved in running this city are on the take." Cummings looked at the prisoners chained to the bench, "When are you planning to talk to them?"

"Whoever hired them must know that we have them. It's a Saturday, so arraignment won't happen until Monday. I think that I'll have one of them taken down to holding."

The chief looked confused, "One of them to holding? What about the other?"

"I'll put him in the interrogation room for a while. Make each of them think the other has turned against them."

"You think that'll work?"

"I won't know until I try." Tiffin lit a cigarette, picked up his phone, and spoke with the duty sergeant. A minute later, two uniformed officers stepped out of the elevator and looked at Tiffin, "Chain one of these two to the table in the interrogation room, put the other in holding."

One of the men spoke up, "What about our phone call? We get a phone call."

Cummings laughed, "You're watching too much of that Perry Mason on TV."

Tiffin grabbed his fedora and looked at Uher, "You want to get some lunch?" Uher nodded.

Cummings looked at the pair, "Where you two going?"

"The Trophy Room, you want to join us?"

"No, I better stay here in case anyone shows up looking for the guys we've got locked up," with his finger, he tamped the tobacco into the bowl of the pipe.

Charlie, the Trophy Room owner and bartender, looked up as the two detectives walked in. "Hey, Tiff. What'll it be?"

"Drop a burger for me with grilled onions. I'll wash it down with a beer."

Uher looked at Tiffin, "Think you could float me for the same? Just until payday."

Tiffin looked down and gently shook his head, "Do the same for my friend here."

"Could I get mayonnaise and green olives instead of the onions?"

Charlie looked to Tiffin, "Deluxe is ten cents more." Tiffin nodded his assent.

The pair sat down and waited for their burgers, "What do you suppose North is up to?" Uher asked as he sipped his beer.

"Probably living the life of Reilly."

Chapter 20

North walked down the shore toward Weiman Road. There was just one cottage between the Pacek's and the road. A thorough check showed the house was secure. He pushed his way through a stand of Elderberry and onto the road; there was no sign of Nelson. "Sonofabitch is hiding somewhere," he thought as he walked back up Oakridge.

Three cigarettes after Majors left, Sheriff Drake pulled up. "What've you got, Brick," he called out as he stepped from his car.

"Majors probably told you that I shot him."

"Yeah, too bad you didn't drop him."

North concurred. "New gun, sights are off just a bit," he responded. Drake wasn't sure if Brick was sincere or not.

"Where's the body?"

"North pointed toward the pickup, "In the bed."

"Have you taken a look at her yet?"

"No, thought it best if there were two of us here."

They walked over to the Ford. North took a corner of the blanket and gently unwound it from the still form that had been Brenda Miller. The red marks around her neck gave grisly testimony to both the last moments of her life and the cause of her death.

"Pretty girl," Drake said as he lit a cigarette. He looked at Brick, "Hard to fathom that this has all happened in just a week. We haven't seen a murder in at least two years, and now three all at once."

"Nelson has gotten too comfortable killing. We've got to stop him; he will kill again."

The sheriff agreed, "He can't go back to the service station. His time there's done."

"True. But he can assume another name, move to another town, and keep right on doing what he's been doing."

Drake looked at North, "Do me a favor, will you?"

"What's that?"

"Next time you get a shot at him, don't miss."

North lit a cigarette and clicked the Zippo closed before answering, "You can take that to the bank."

Five minutes later, the coroner pulled up; blue smoke came from his forty-nine Ford's tailpipe. North motioned him over to the pickup. "Hello, Doc. Meet nineteen-year-old Brenda Miller."

Von Boren shook his head, "Poor child." He gave the body a quick examination, "She's in full rigor, so death occurred between twelve and twenty-four hours ago. The cause of death would appear to be the same as the other two. I'll know more after I can fully examine her."

While Von Boren made notes about the Miller girl's body and took a few photographs, Drake and North made another pass through the house. After the house, they gave the truck a thorough going over. There was nothing that stood out in either. The hearse from the mortuary finally arrived to transport the body to the morgue. North watched as they drove away, "I'll take Pacek's truck back to the office if that's okay with you?" North asked the sheriff.

"You can ride with me if you want. You said you'd taken the coil wire, so Nelson can't slip back around and take the truck."

"He's not a dumb kid, no matter what his uncle says. Taking the coil wire was just to slow him down. He can pull a plug wire and run it between the coil and distributor. The truck will run rough, but it'll drive."

"You have the keys?"

"I won't need them." At that, North opened the hood of the truck and replaced the coil wire. Stepping into the cab, he reached under the dashboard and pulled the wires from the back of the ignition switch. North twisted two of them together and depressed the starter; the engine fired up.

Drake looked impressed, "Do I want to know how you learned that?"

"France. A few of us liberated a car the Jerrys left behind. A kid from New Jersey taught us how to do it."

North sat down in the Ford and put the truck into gear. Backing out of the drive, he followed Drake to Weiman Road to return to Howell. Half a mile from Pacek's cottage, Jimmy Nelson peered from behind some bushes and watched his ride to freedom go past; a dirty red shop rag was tied around his right upper arm. The rag was saturated in blood.

Back at the Sheriff's Office, Brick added a few notes to his file before calling Al Pacek, letting him know he could claim his pickup. While he was busy doing that, Drake was calling the State Police for reinforcements.

"Every State Trooper that can be spared will be searching the Putnam township area for Nelson," Drake said as he stepped from his office.

Crushing his cigarette, North looked at the Sheriff, "He can't get far. He'll need a place he can hole up. Depending on how badly I wounded him, he also might need medical attention. We should get hold of every doctor and veterinarian around there and let them know to keep an eye out."

"Good idea. I'll get Joyce on that."

North stood, "Okay, I'm going to grab my truck and keep looking for Nelson."

"You can take one of our cars."

"There's going to be plenty of marked cars crisscrossing Putnam township. My old pickup shouldn't attract much attention."

"Okay. That makes sense. Check in as you can."

North crushed the Bradmore onto his head, "Will do." The door to the parking lot had almost closed behind him when Joyce called his name. He turned and reentered the building. "What's up?"

"Just took a call for you from the University Hospital. They say they need to know how to get hold of Miss Kingston's family."

"Crap! I should have run by the cottage and gotten her purse when I was down there."

Joyce cocked her head slightly, "You have a lady-friend in the hospital and her purse at your cottage?"

"Long story. Did they leave a number?" He reached for a piece of paper that Joyce handed him, "Thanks, doll."

"I want that long story when you get back, Deputy North."

"Yes, ma'am." He made a half-hearted attempt at both a salute and to seem nonchalant.

Joyce noticed his tension, "I've only known you for a week, but you don't seem like your normal self."

"Sylvia is a friend from LaSalle Harbor. She was on her way to Detroit to see her parents and decided to stop off in Ann Arbor for the weekend."

"To see you?"

"Yes. She wasn't feeling well when she got off the train yesterday. This morning when I left, she was asleep. When Majors and I ran by my place later this morning, she was so out of it we drove her to the hospital."

"Let me know if there's anything I can do to help," Joyce put her hand on his arm.

"Thank you. I need to check if she's got an address book in her purse and then get hold of the hospital."

"Give me back that note," she said as she reached for the paper she had handed him moments before. "Let me write my home number down. In case you need someone to talk to."

"I'll be fine," he said as she grabbed the note from his hand and scratched a few numbers on the back of it.

Augustine Meijer "Murder in Hell"

"Here! I don't go giving my number to every man who comes along. So consider yourself special."

Under normal circumstances, Brick would have had some witty repartee. This afternoon the best he could do was to mutter "Thanks" on his way out the door.

The drive to the cottage was a blur; North's thoughts moved between Sylvia, their time together, and Jimmy Nelson. He pulled into the driveway of North's End without any real memory of how he got there. Gatto was waiting for him; the cat pushed past him as soon as the door swung open. "Got nothing for you, bub," North said as he turned Sylvia's purse out onto the table. There among the Lifesavers, bobby pins, and tissues, was a small red leatherette address book. He flipped through the pages and found no listing for Kingston. Confused for just a moment, he opened the book at the 'M' tab; sure enough, there was a listing for Mom and Dad. He pushed the book into his jacket pocket.

North looked at the cat, who was busy cleaning himself on the sofa. "You planning on staying there?" he asked. Gatto never looked up. "Suit yourself." Grabbing his hat, North pulled the door closed behind himself and walked to the truck. The mile and a half drive into Hell seemed to take as long as the trip down from the Sheriff's office. He stopped in front of the general store and walked up to the payphone.

He lifted the receiver and dialed 'O."

"Operator," a nasal voice responded.

"Operator, I need Ann Arbor, WEbster 6-4000."

"Please deposit twenty-five cents for the first three minutes."

North dug in his pocket and pulled out a quarter, which he dropped into the slot. Within moments, he heard the phone ring on the other end.

"University Hospital. How may I direct your call?"

North looked at the note that Joyce had given him, "I need to speak with Doctor Pritchard. Tell him it's about Sylvia Kingston."

"Let me page him. Please hold."

He pulled the last cigarette out of the package and lit it. He read the motto on the pack, "*In Hoc Signo Vinces*," "In this sign, you will conquer." The Bell Telephone operator returned, "Please deposit fifteen-cents for the next three minutes." He pulled a dime and a nickel from his pocket and dropped them into the appropriate slots on the top of the phone. He had just finished doing so when a male voice came on the phone, "This is Doctor Prichard."

"Doc, this is Richard North. I brought Sylvia Kingston to the hospital late this morning."

"Yes, Mr. North. I was hoping you found a number for Miss Kingston's family."

"You ready for it?"

"Yes. Go ahead."

North read the number to the doctor, who then repeated it. "How is she, Doc?"

"She's a very sick woman, Mr. North."

"I don't need a medical degree to know that," North growled. "I'm asking how she is."

"We're having trouble bringing her fever down. She's awakened a couple of times in a confused and agitated state. When she is awake, she keeps repeating that her neck hurts. I've ordered a test to rule out Bacterial Meningitis."

"What's that?"

"Meningitis is an infection of the meninges. The lining keeps the brain and skull from rubbing each other. Was she complaining about head or neck pain before you brought her in?"

"Yes. She had a terrible headache and said her neck hurt last night. What kind of test are you going to do?"

"I've ordered a spinal tap. We'll gather spinal fluid and check it for bacteria."

"And if you find this bacteria, what's next?"

"Sulphonamides administered intravenously."

North sputtered, "Sulfa? The best you can do is Sulfa? We had that in the war. Haven't you guys come up with anything better in all these years?"

"Research into synthetic antibiotics is ongoing. Now, if you don't mind, I'd like to call her family."

North crushed the cigarette under his foot, "Is she going to get better?"

"We're doing everything we can."

In the general store, North picked up another carton of Pall Malls. Opening the carton and lighting one, he called the office. The phone was answered on the second ring, "Livingston County Sheriff's Office."

"Joyce, it's Brick. Any news on locating Nelson?"

"Nothing. The State boys are going door-to-door out from the Pacek cottage," the now-familiar gruff voice replied. "Where are you?"

"At the general store in Hell. It's the closest phone to my cottage."

"How's your lady friend?"

North picked a piece of loose tobacco off his lip, "Sylvia, her name is Sylvia. The doctor says she's really sick."

"I'm sorry. Hope she gets better quickly. Where are you going to be?"

"I'll head back to Hi-Land Lake, see if I can coordinate with the state troopers. Where's Sheriff Drake?"

"The Sheriff and three of our guys are down there somewhere now."

"Okay. I'll see if I can't find them." North took a drag on the cigarette. "Thanks for your help." He hung up the receiver and walked back to the pickup. Sitting behind the wheel, he took a moment to realize that hard as it was to believe, it was still Saturday. He looked at his watch; it was a quarter past four. The sun would set in ninety minutes.

Less than ten minutes later, he was following Weiman Road around the south end of Hi-Land Lake. About a half-mile up from his cottage on Hickman Court, he saw the distinctive Blue Goose color Michigan State Police car parked on the side of the road. He parked behind it and opened his door. The trooper didn't allow him out of his vehicle, "I need you to stay in your truck," the trooper hollered as he stepped from his car, hand on the revolver hanging from his Sam Browne belt.

North placed his hands on the steering wheel as the trooper approached, "My name's North. I'm with the Livingston County Sheriff's office."

"Step out and show me some ID."

He carefully stepped out of the Dodge and pulled the Mackinaw back to reveal the badge on his belt, "Satisfied?"

"We're searching for a fugitive. I've been asked to keep people from going down here."

"I understand. I'm trying to locate Sheriff Drake. Any idea where I might find them?" North lit a cigarette.

"Let me see," the trooper stepped back to the new 1957 Chevy four-door. "Car seven-nine, car seven-nine to Lieutenant Whitehead. Over." North heard the radio crackle before a voice responded, "Whitehead, what have you got? Over."

"I have a county cop down here that needs to locate the Sheriff, over."

Again, the crackled of the radio preceded the voice, "Drake's here with me. We're about a quarter-mile further down the road. He wants to know if it's North you've got with you. Over."

The trooper looked up from the Motorola radio in his car, "Your name North?"

"That's me."

"Lieutenant, yes, I've got North here. Over."

"Send him down. Over."

"Okay, deputy. They're just down the road a bit."

North tipped his fedora, "Thank you. Over."

The trooper displayed the merest hint of a smile, "Funny man, huh?"

North turned toward the pickup, "Not usually." It was less than two minutes before he saw both the brown and white of a Livingston sheriff's vehicle and the blue State Police car. He parked the truck on the opposite side of the road and walked over. "How much has been searched?"

Drake nodded to North, "Brick, let me introduce you to Lieutenant Phil Whitehead. Phil and I met in the Pacific." North shook the offered hand.

"The Sheriff has told me a bit about you. Seems you're on kind of a bus driver's holiday."

"Yeah, all my luck. Come to the country for some quiet and end up in a murder investigation."

"From what Tom's told me, trouble seems to follow you. Any truth to that?"

North shook his head, "More truth than fiction. So, where have you searched?"

Drake spoke first, "We've checked most, if not all, the cottages and outbuildings around this side of the lake."

Whitehead nodded toward the south, "I've got men down on Territorial Road, which is about a mile and a half from here, checking for Nelson. Also, have a dog working his way through the marsh between here and there."

"Weird, isn't it?" North said, scratching the back of his head. "I lived walking distance from a Territorial Road in LaSalle Harbor, and there's one here too."

The State Police Lieutenant looked at North, "It's the same road. Runs from Detroit all the way across the state to the Harbor. Follows the old St. Joseph trail first laid down by the Sauk and Potawatomi."

North was impressed, "You know your history."

"I've been with the State Police since I was discharged by the Marines. I don't know much history, but I know the roads of southern Michigan.

"Where do you need me?" North looked between the Sheriff and the Lieutenant.

Chapter 21

Tiffin and Uher stepped into the interrogation room and sat opposite their prisoner in the green coveralls. Tiffin pulled a pack of cigarettes from his pocket, slowly drew one out, and rolled it between his fingers for a minute. He put the filter between his lips and dug in his pocket for a box of matches. His motions were deliberate and paced. After what felt like several minutes, he finally struck a match and lit the cigarette. He held the match up and watched it burn, putting it out only as the flame finally reached his fingers. Only then did he take a deep drag on the Lucky Strike and slowly blow the smoke from between his lips.

"You gonna ask me a question or make love to that fucking cigarette?"

Tiff looked across at the man who was chained to the table, "What's your hurry? You're not going anywhere that I know of."

"I make a phone call, and I'll be out of here in five minutes," the prisoner said with enough arrogance to tell the detectives that he was probably telling the truth.

"Here's the deal," Tiffin took another drag on the cigarette, "you won't be arraigned until Monday. Bail, if there is any, won't be decided upon until then. So, I hope you brought your toothbrush because you're not going anywhere."

"Then transfer me over to the county jail. I don't want to be held here."

Tiffin looked to Uher, "Dan, this guy doesn't like our cooler. He prefers to be transferred to the county for safekeeping."

"Maybe they've got softer cots," Uher joked.

"Maybe they've got better coffee," Tiffin scratched his temple. "Or maybe, just maybe, Clyde here thinks he'll get better treatment at the county jail." Barry gave the man a severe looking over. "What did you say your name was?"

"I didn't."

Tiffin thought for a few minutes as he studied the man's face. "I know you!" he finally announced.

"Yeah, I don't think so."

"No. I do know you. R.W., you work for Red Wilson," Tiffin said, referring to the county sheriff. "You're one of his deputies." Tiffin was sure he saw the man swallow hard.

"I don't know what you're talking about."

"Save it." He turned to Uher, "Come on, Dan, let's go have a chat with his partner." The two detectives stood and walked to the door.

"You can't hold me here!"

Uher looked at his partner, "Did you hear something, Tiff?"

"No, why?" Tiffin pulled the door shut behind him. The two took the elevator to the basement. They could still hear the cursing as the elevator doors slid shut.

In addition to the building's physical plant, the Safety Buildings basement held four holding cells and a small interrogation room. An older officer sat guard on the cells. He was working the crossword from the newspaper. "Hey Lou," Tiffin said as they stepped out of the elevator, "how's it going?"

"Saturday's puzzles are almost as bad as they get. Of course, Sunday's the worst. I need a nine-letter word for mulish."

"Stubborn," Uher offered.

Lou shook his head, "Nope, that's only eight."

"Obstinate," Tiffin said as he looked over the officer's shoulder.

"That's it! Now, what can I do for you, detectives?"

"Need to chat with your prisoner in coveralls. You want to bring him to the interrogation room?" Lou nodded, stood, and walked to the barred door the led into the corridor of cells.

The detectives walked into the interrogation room and turned on the buzzing fluorescent light on the ceiling. The light had just stopped flickering when Lou brought the prisoner in and chained him to the tabletop.

Uher stood behind the man in green, Tiffin sat down opposite him. "How are we treating you, deputy?" The man's pallor took on an ashen color. "Oh, it's not your fault; your partner told us you work for Sheriff Wilson. Isn't that right, Detective Uher."

"That's right, Detective Tiffin."

"So, let's cut through the bullshit, shall we?" Tiffin pulled his notepad and a pencil from his pocket, "Your partner was more concerned about covering his own ass than protecting yours. He says that you recruited him for this little caper today."

Color returned to the man's face. This time it was red, "That's bullshit. I didn't want to do this at all, but Ray said it would get us in good with the Sheriff."

"So, you're saying Wilson recruited Ray and Ray recruited you?"

"I don't know who recruited Ray, but I was just along for the ride."

Uher shook his head, "It's tough to believe anything you say, considering we caught you trying to steal evidence."

"Who wanted the books that Oftermatt was keeping?"

"I think I better keep my mouth shut."

Tiffin smiled to himself and remembered a line that North frequently used, "The water gets deep pretty quick, doesn't it? Who wanted the evidence stolen?"

The deputy looked down, "I'm afraid of the people who want that information."

"If I were you, I'd be more afraid of what the men in the State Pen will do to you when they find out you were a cop."

The deputy suddenly broke down and began to sob, "You gotta help me."

Tiffin picked up the pencil, "Why don't we start with your name and Ray's last name."

"My name is Getz, Art Getz. Ray is Raymond George."

"Thank you, Art," Tiffin put his hand on the deputy's forearm, "I know that was hard. Where were you supposed to take the stuff you found?"

"We were supposed to take it to the District Attorney's Office. Someone was supposed to meet us there." Getz looked down and studied his hands.

Tiffin brought his hand down hard on the metal desk, causing both Getz and Uher to jump, "Who? Who was supposed to meet you there?"

"I swear I don't know. I'm guessing it must be the District Attorney himself. Who else would use his office?"

"That would be my guess," Uher agreed.

"Detective, my wife is probably standing on her ear. Do you think I can call her?"

Tiffin closed his notepad, "I'll get back to you on that." He raised his voice to be heard through the metal door, "Lou!"

The officer opened the door, "Detective?"

"See that Mr. Getz gets back to his cell and see if you can't find him some chow."

"You got it. Hey, before you go. What's a four-letter word for taradiddler?"

Uher looked confused, "That a crossword clue?"

"Liar," Tiffin said, "Like what I hope Art Getz isn't." Once back on the second floor, Tiffin walked into the Chief's office and closed the door.

Cummings clenched his pipe between his teeth, "What've you come up with?"

In a low voice, Tiffin answered, "We're up shit creek. Our two clowns both work for the Sheriff."

"Red?" Cummings jumped to his feet, the chair he was sitting in banged into the credenza behind his desk, knocking a picture of Mrs. Cummings over. "How far does this go?"

"After burgling Oftermatts' office, they were supposed to take the evidence to the District Attorney."

Cummings shook his head, "The Mayor, the Sheriff, the DA. Fuck, this is a conspiracy."

"What now?"

"I don't know who we can trust. Our only choice is the FBI. Where's the evidence you collected?"

Tiffin used his forehead to point to his desk, "Locked in my desk."

"I want that locked in my safe right now before anyone gets the idea to come looking for it. Grab it while I call the Bureau and bring it in here. Then get hold of the Duty Sergeant and have him station two men outside this office around the clock. And have them issued shotguns from the armory."

"You think that's necessary?"

"I think desperate men do desperate things." Cummings picked up his phone and waited just a moment for the switchboard to answer, "This is the Chief. Get me the FBI Field Office in Detroit."

Chapter 22

Worried, tired, hungry, and in need of a stiff drink, North pulled onto Hickman Court and turned into the drive of North's End. He stepped out of the pickup and stretched; the sun had been down for ninety-minutes. The search had been called for darkness.

As he approached the front step, Gatto began doing figure eights around his legs. "Hey bub," North muttered as he fumbled for the key to the front door. He stopped and looked at the marmalade-colored cat he had left on the sofa five hours before. "How the fuck did you get out?" North used the side of his foot to push the cat aside before removing the Colt from its holster. Reaching for the doorknob, he found the door locked. Quietly, he inserted the key and pushed the door inward. The room was pitch black.

North sensed the motion to his right about the same time that something heavy crashed down on his head, sending the Bradmore flying. North, stunned by the blow, dropped to a knee, tucked his left shoulder, and rolled away from his attacker.

As his eyes adjusted to the darkness, he saw the silhouette of the man who'd hit him coming forward. North regained his balance and fired at what he believed to be the man's center mass. The flash from the barrel of the gun illuminated Jimmy Nelson and temporarily blinded North. Knowing the room as well as he did, North rolled over the back of the sofa and made it to the wall switch in the kitchen, causing the light over the sink to come to life. Nelson, bleeding from a belly wound and holding an ax over his head, lunged at North. A single shot rang out from the .38, and a red dot appeared in the center of Nelson's forehead. The standing corpse of the rapist-murderer stood perfectly still for a moment before it dropped the ax and fell forward.

North staggered back and dropped into a kitchen chair. Blood flowed from a wound on the back of his head that adrenaline was preventing him from feeling. As he sat, the room began to spin. He realized that he was sliding off the chair but was powerless to do anything about it.

Three hours later, he woke cold and with a crushing headache. Gatto had curled up at his side and stirred as North moved. "Crap," he said as he reached for the back of his head. His hand encountered both dried blood and a flap of skin that should not have been there. "What the hell?" he asked as he looked at the ax on the floor next to Nelson's body. "Sonofabitch," he muttered as he pushed himself first to his knees and then onto his feet. His head pounded with every step as he walked into the bathroom.

He grabbed a washcloth, wet it, and held it to the wound. Burning pain brought every nerve in his body alive. He dabbed at the damage, rinsed the cloth, and gingerly used it to probe the place where the ax had encountered his skull. North was pleased to find that nothing gave as he pressed, "Good," he said aloud, "at least he didn't crack my head open."

North wrapped an old dishtowel around his head and went to survey the main room of the house. Nelson's body lay where it had dropped. The ax had hair and blood on it. North realized that both belonged to him. The Bradmore sat next to the coffee table; its back was cut where the ax had sliced through it.

The Bulova on his wrist showed it to be half-past ten. He reached into his pant pocket; his keys weren't there. Looking to the open front door, he found them still hanging in the knob.

"Okay, Gatto. Time to go." He gingerly reached down, grabbed the cat under the ribcage, and carried him out the door. Locking the door, he walked over to the Dodge and sat in it for a few moments before backing out of the drive. The mile and a half drive into Hell seemed to take longer than it should have. A teenage boy was leaning against the general store wall, the receiver of the payphone pressed between his shoulder and ear.

"Get off the phone, kid," North said as he stepped onto the curb.

"Screw you," he said in North's direction. Then into the phone, "I don't know, just some old man who wants to use the phone."

"I'm going to be polite just one more time. Hang up."

The teen turned to confront North. On seeing the blood, bandage, and badge, he quickly complied and hung up after shouting into the receiver, "Gotta go."

North shouldered the youth aside, picked up the receiver, and dialed zero.

"Operator," a nasal voice answered.

"Connect me with the Sheriff's Office."

The phone rang half a dozen times before it was answered by an unfamiliar, sleepy male voice, "Livingston County Sheriff."

"Listen carefully. This is Deputy North. I need you to get the Sheriff and Coroner to my cottage as quickly as possible."

"What's this about?"

"It's about you doing what I'm telling you to do. And tell the doctor to bring his bag. I'm going to need some stitching up."

"I don't want to wake the Sheriff unless there's a good reason."

"There's a dead man in my living room. Is that good enough for you?"

"Uh, okay."

"Repeat what I've told you."

"Deputy North. The Sheriff and Coroner to go to your cottage. Dead man in your living room. Tell Doc to bring his bag."

North hung up and turned to the teen who was still standing in front of the store. He reached in his pocket, grabbed a dime, and put it on top of the phone. "Thanks, kid."

"There's a dead guy in your living room? That's like on the beam!"

Trying to decipher the slang, North climbed back into the pickup and turned toward the cottage. His head screamed, and he was wracked by nausea. Once back at North's End, he stayed in the truck and smoked a few cigarettes as he waited. Gatto circled the pickup. North finally opened the door, "Come on, bub. It's warm in here." The cat jumped in and laid on the bench seat next to North. "You're extra chummy tonight, bub."

A tap on the drivers' side window awakened him from a nap he didn't realize that he had taken. Drake and Von Boren were both standing next to the Dodge.

"What the hell happened to you?" Drake asked.

"Think I got hit in the head with an ax," North said as he slid out of the truck.

Von Boren put his hand on North's arm, "Why don't we go in and let me look at your head?"

Drake looked to Brick, "Who's the dead guy you referred to?"

"Nelson," North grunted.

"Nelson? What the hell was he doing in your cottage?"

"I must have left the door unlocked when I ran through here earlier. Nelson found the door open when he was looking for a place to hide. Walked in, locked the door, and hunkered down."

"So when the state boys were checking cottages…"

North finished the Sheriff's sentence, "The door was locked, and the blinds were drawn, so they just moved along."

The scene in the cottage was more gruesome than North had expected. There was blood where he had been hit and more blood where he had first shot Nelson. Nelson's body was surrounded by blood and brain matter, and there was a pool of blood where North had laid.

"Quite the blood bath," Drake observed.

Von Boren paid little attention to the room or the body, "Sit down, let me look at your head."

North did as he was directed.

"Pretty ragged wound," the doctor said as he poured saline on the back of North's head. I was expecting more of a clean cut.

North looked at his fedora, "I think my hat saved my noggin."

The doctor walked over and examined the hat, "The ax must have slipped against the felt when it hit the back of your head and caused it to slide down. You're a lucky man, North."

Von Boren cleaned and shook sulfa powder into the wound before he stitched and dress it. "You done this before?" North asked as the doctor wrapped gauze around his head.

"A time or two," Von Boren said as he began packing his bag. "I spent most of my time working in a field hospital in Italy during the war."

Brick sat on a kitchen chair and recounted the fight that had taken place. As Drake listened, he lit a cigarette and offered one to Brick.

"Mind handing me that bottle?" North asked the sheriff, who was leaning against the kitchen counter. Drake picked up the Old Quaker, pulled the cork, and handed it over. North took a deep pull and handed it back to Drake, who did the same.

"Hell of a week, Brick," Drake wiped his mouth with the back of his shirt sleeve. He looked at Von Boren, "Should we get my deputy to a hospital?"

Von Boren shook his head, "I don't think that's necessary. But I am concerned that he has a concussion. Can you get someone out here to spend the night, just in case he develops complications?"

North looked at Von Boren, "What kind of complications?"

"Dizzyness, confusion, agitation."

North tried to laugh, but it hurt too much, "Sounds like a typical night of drinking."

"Except the headache is going to be far worse in the morning than a typical hangover," the doctor closed his bag and stood.

"You don't know my hangovers."

Drake took a deep pull on his cigarette. He looked at Von Boren, "I'll babysit him. Do me a favor, though. When you get back into town, call my wife and let her know where I am."

North looked at Drake, "Well if you're going to be here, you might as well get a fire going. And someone let that cat out of my truck." Another thirty minutes passed before the mortuary came for the body. The three men sat in silence.

"Leave him at the morgue," the coroner told the ambulance drivers. "I won't examine him until tomorrow afternoon." Then to Drake, "Pretty much just have to write the report. I know the cause of death."

"By the book, Doc. By the book," Drake said as Von Boren walked out behind the men from the mortuary. "Okay, North. Where do you hide the coffee, and whose cat is this?"

"There's a bag of coffee in the cabinet to the left of the sink, and I have no idea who the cat belongs to."

By the time Drake had filled the percolator with water and coffee and sat it on the stove, North had fallen asleep on the sofa. Gatto jumped onto the couch and curled up next to Brick. "By the looks of it," Drake whispered at the cat, "I'd say you're his cat."

Chapter 23

Chief Cummings nervously sat in his office smoking his pipe. Tiffin and Uher were each occupying one of the green leather chairs on the opposite side of the oak desk. Suddenly, Cummings stood, "You boys are married, right?"

Tiffin and Uher looked at each other. Tiffin spoke first, "Yeah, why?"

"I'm just thinking these men are anxious and eager to get their hands on what we have. I wouldn't put it past them to use your families as leverage."

"My wife and I are separated," Uher piped in.

"Doesn't matter. Call them. Tell them that a police car will be there to pick them up within the next thirty minutes. Have them pack just what they need."

"Where are you taking them?" Tiffin asked. The concern in his tone was unmistakable.

"At the moment, I can't think of a safer place than here. Now, get on the horn and call your wives."

At their desks, both detectives picked up their phones. Tiffin spoke to the operator, "This is Detective Tiffin. Get me Walnut 5-9181." Uher made a similar call.

By the sixth ring, Tiffin was getting nervous. Finally, Kaye picked up, "Hello?"

"Kaye, no time to explain. Get Ben and Hannah dressed, grab toothbrushes, and whatever else you think they need. A police car will be there shortly to bring you here."

"Barry, what's going on?" Kaye's voice was edgy.

"Please, just do what I ask."

Headlights swept past the living room window, "A car just pulled into the drive. Is that the one you're talking about already?"

"No! Grab the kids and get to the tornado room. Now! I'll be right there. Now go."

"Chief, it looks like someone is already at my house!" Tiffin called across the office. Cummings picked up the phone on his desk, "This is the chief. Get me the duty sergeant."

"Right away, Chief," the operator responded.

"Sergeant Nichelson."

"Nick, this is the chief. Send everything you've got to," he looked at Tiffin, "what's your address?"

"Five twenty-two Hunter," Tiffin was pulling on his jacket.

Cumming continued, "Five twenty-two Hunter. Detective Tiffin's house is being broken into."

"Right away, chief!" Nichelson hung up the phone and keyed the microphone on the counter. A yellow lamp on the Motorola radio in every car lit up, "Attention all cars, attention all cars. Five twenty-two Hunter, Five two two Hunter. Officer's family in distress. Do not stop to call in. Converge there."

Kaye and the kids huddled in the corner of the cold room under the front stoop. A wooden bookcase was attached to the front of the metal door that separated the cold room from the den. The bookcase blended in with the wooden paneling of the room. The latch that opened the door was difficult to find, even if one knew what they were looking for. Kaye had accused her husband of reading too many spy novels when he was installing it. At the moment, she was glad that he did.

From their hiding place, they could clearly hear the sound of the front door being forced open. Heavy footsteps pounded on the ceiling above them. Kaye held her children and gently put her hands over their mouths. "I need you to be as quiet as you've ever been," she whispered. Hannah, just six, let out a small whimper.

"It'll be okay," her eight-year-old brother whispered. "Dad's coming."

"There's no one upstairs!" a husky male voice was heard saying. "Beds have been slept in; shoes and coats are here. Keep looking!" Feet pounded their way down the basement steps, "They gotta be here somewhere. Hey, someone check the garage and backyard!"

It sounded like two men were making their way through the basement. One of them banged his head on the ductwork leading off of the furnace in the laundry room on the other side of the wall from the den. Kaye held her children tighter, "Shhh, she whispered." She could hear them in the den outside the door. "Where the hell are they?" the voice said. He sounded inches from her ear. "Come on, let's see if they ran to a neighbor's house."

They heard the footsteps go up the stairs and into the living room. Suddenly they heard an amplified voice, "This is the police. Come out with your hands up."

"Can we go now, mommy?" Benjamin whispered, the bravery now slipping away.

"No, Ben," Kaye comforted him, "Let's stay here until your dad comes to get us."

The two men in the house recognized they were outnumbered and outgunned. Both surrendered as they looked down the barrels of a half dozen shotguns. They were quickly handcuffed.

"Anyone else with you?" Tiffin asked as he walked up to his own front door.

"Do you see anyone else?" the man with the husky voice responded.

Tiffin struck him across the cheek with the butt of his gun, "Answer my question!"

"There are two more. They went to check outside and the neighbors' places." Even with blood on his cheek, the man was laughing, "Your holding cells are going to get pretty full. I'd be nervous if I was housing all of us."

About that time, two blue State Police cars came rushing down the street, the red gumball lamps on their roofs rotating. Tiffin grinned, "Oh, sorry. You're heading to the State Police Post in Niles. I won't have to put up with your smell."

Tiffin raced through the house and down to the basement. "Kaye!" he shouted as he came down the stairs. He released the catch on the bookcase, but the door did not move. He said the password, "Cucumber!" Kaye unlatched the door from the inside.

"Oh, Barry!" she cried as she and the children came out from the cold, dark space. "What's going on?"

"Let's get the kids to the car, and I'll tell you," He hugged them all; a tear rolled down his cheek. She whispered in his ear, "I'm sorry I made fun of you and your spy saferoom."

"I'm glad I didn't let you talk me out of it."

Kaye looked into her husband's eyes. "One thing Mr. Bond," she said, referring to the spy character in the books Tiffin enjoyed.

"What's that?" he smiled.

"Can we put some comfortable mats on the floor in there? That concrete is hard!"

"Yes, Miss Moneypenny." Tiffin laughed.

Kaye whispered into his ear, "Call me Eve."

"You know, in the books, they never, uh," he looked at his children, "get together."

"Good thing this isn't a book."

Once Tiffin secured the front door the best he could, and with a police escort, he brought his family to the Safety Building. Stepping out of the elevator, he spied Cummings at his desk. Two armed officers flanked the door. "Did Uher get hold of his wife?"

Cummings shook his head, "Turns out she's in Ludington visiting an aunt."

"Where's Uher now?"

"Asleep in the interrogation room. He and I will take turns covering my office." Cummings looked at the children in their pajamas and slippers, "Hi kids, remember me?" Hannah shook her head and took up a safe position behind her father.

Ben whispered to his sister, "It's Uncle Pete; he only looks scary."

Tiffin and Kaye got the kids bedded down in the day room. She left the door ajar so that a bit of light entered, "Mommy is right outside if you need me."

"You going to try to get some sleep?" Tiffin asked his wife.

"Are you kidding?! I don't know if I'll ever fall asleep again. Now, who were those men, and why did they break into our house?" Tiffin sat her at his desk and told her everything he felt he could.

The sun rose above the horizon at 7:04 AM the morning of Sunday, October twentieth. Tiffin walked to the DuBois bakery across Main Street from the Safety Building. There he purchased two jelly-filled doughnuts for the kids and a small coffee cake for himself and Kaye.

Two men in dark suits, white shirts, and dark ties were in Cummings' office when he arrived upstairs. "Tiffin, these men are from the FBI. Help me go over what we know with them."

Tiffin gave the baked goods to his wife and closed the door to the Chief's office as he stepped inside. It was almost ninety minutes before the door opened again. He walked over to Kaye, "I'm going to get a uniformed officer to take you home. Call your brother in South Bend and see if you three can spend a few days with him and his family."

"Barry, why?"

"Because I don't know how things are going to shake out. I'd feel better if I knew you, Ben, and Hannah are safe."

"I don't like it. I'd rather have you close."

Tiffin nodded his understanding. "You call me when you get there." He leaned down and kissed his wife on the forehead, "I love you."

The FBI agents left right behind Kaye and the children. They took with them the two deputies from the holding cells along with the box of evidence.

Cummings saw them to the door before returning to the squad room. "Been a long night," he said as he took a cigarette off Tiffin.

"Has it only been one night? Feels like a month."

"It does," the chief blew smoke toward the ceiling, "and it's not over yet."

Chapter 24

Sunlight and a full bladder woke North. He was stretched out on the old sofa in the living room. Laying there a while, he tried to recall the events of the night before. Lifting his head brought the reality of the wound on the back of his skull. He smelled coffee before he noticed Drake sitting at the kitchen table.

"Ouch," North gently lifted his head off the pillow. "Tom? How long you been sitting there?"

"All night. How're you feeling?

"Like the Chrysler building dropped a steel gargoyle on my head." Brick swung his feet onto the floor and pushed himself into a seated position.

"The doc told me that you're lucky to be alive. If that ax had been half an inch closer to the middle of your head, you'd have left in that hearse last night instead of Nelson." Drake lit a cigarette and offered one to North, who gladly took it.

There was orange cat hair on the front of the Mac. North brushed it off, "Did the cat sleep on me or something?"

"That cat of yours didn't leave your side until the sun came up."

"He's not my cat," North argued.

"You better let him know that. I tried to move him out in the middle of the night, and the little bastard hissed at me."

Brick stood and immediately fell back into a seated position, "Feels like my brain is loose." Drake offered him a hand that was not accepted. "No, I got this," North said as he willed himself to stand.

Once in the bathroom, North gently peeled away the bandages and examined his head as best he could. His hand touched the dried blood that saturated the back of his scalp. He could feel how swollen the area was around the wound. Carefully closing Sylvia's cosmetic bag, he took it into the bedroom and put it on the floor next to her suitcase. Grabbing some clean clothes, North walked back through the main room and into the bath. He called out to Drake, "Why don't you go home? I'm going to clean up and drive down to the University to check on my friend."

"You sure you're okay?"

"I'll be fine." North closed the bathroom door and turned on the space heater. He heard Drake close the front door and his vehicle crank over. The hot shower loosened his muscles. He carefully washed the blood out of his hair and climbed out of the tub with utmost caution. After shaving, he examined the clothes that he'd worn the night before. He left his shirt and the Mac soaking in cold water before he got dressed.

He pulled on his gray suit and looked for his fedora before he remembered its demise. Hatless, he walked out to the pickup and headed back to Ann Arbor. Traffic was slight on Sunday morning, and he was parked outside the University Hospital within forty minutes.

The woman at the information window scrutinized him, "Do you need a doctor?"

"No, I'm here to visit Miss Sylvia Kingston. I'm not certain what room she's in."

"Let me check," she flipped through the Rolodex on her desk, "Miss Kingston is in room seven twenty. Do you need directions?"

"I think I can find the seventh floor," North said as he walked away to find an elevator. Unfortunately, the first elevator he stepped into only went to the fifth floor. The elevator operator directed him to the east wing, where he located a car that took him to the seventh floor. He walked up to the nurses' station, "Where's room seven twenty?"

Without looking at him, the nurse tilted her head to the right, "Down the hall on your right." North had just stepped away when the nurse looked up, "Sir! Maybe you should sit down."

North turned abruptly, "Why?!"

"You've got a weeping wound on the back of your head."

"I'm well aware of the state of my noggin."

"Why don't you let me dress that before you get blood on something, or worse, an infection."

He gave her offer a moment of thought before prudently accepting, "The doctor already has me stitched up. I should be fine."

"And did the doctor leave your head unbandaged?"

"No, I took them off before I showered."

"You washed your head?"

"I needed to get the blood off."

The nurse shook her head, "You know, that blood clot is half of what's holding your scalp together. Those stitches are only doing part of the job."

She led him into a small room and pulled out a stool, "Sit down, let's look at this." She examined the wound, and the row of stitches, "Whoever did this knows what he's doing."

"He was a combat surgeon." North winced as she used peroxide to wash the area around the gash.

"I wonder if I know him. I served in combat hospitals during the war." With that, she dusted the area with sulfa, applied a heavy layer of gauze, and wrapped his head in a white bandage.

"Doc Steve Von Boren from Howell."

"Nope, don't know him." She took a stainless tray and held it in front of North, "What do you think?"

North chuckled, "I look like Claude Rains."

"Yeah, but you're not invisible. Quite the opposite. So how did a good-looking man like you come up with a head wound like this?"

"I used my head to stop an ax."

"I wouldn't do that again."

"I'll try to remember that."

The room Syliva occupied had three beds; two were occupied. Sylvia was in the one closest to the window. An elderly woman was in the bed opposite hers in the alcove created by the restroom. Both women were asleep. A rubber IV tube extended from a glass bottle hanging from a metal stand to the inside of her right wrist. North read the label, "Sulphonamides Solution."

He pulled the metal chair closer to the bed and put his hand on hers. She was warm, and that warmth brought him some comfort. He sat there long enough that he began to nap. He was awakened by a young doctor who walked in.

"Goodness, I didn't realize anyone was in here. Sorry to disturb you. I just want to check on Miss Kingston."

North yawned, "I had a rough night. Guess I fell asleep."

The doctor looked at the bandages around North's head, "Looks like a rough night. Car accident?"

"Just another day on the job," North pulled back his jacket to reveal the badge on his belt. "How's Sylvia?"

"Family?" the doctor asked.

"As close as it gets," North didn't consider it a lie.

"We ruled out Poliomyelitis pretty early on. We just got the results back from the spinal tap about an hour ago. Miss Kingston definitely has bacterial meningitis."

North lit a cigarette, "I don't understand. How would she have gotten that?"

"The simple answer is bacteria got into her blood and traveled to her brain."

"What kind of bacteria?"

"It's called Neisseria. It's actually pretty common, and most people can fight it off. They might feel like they're getting a cold."

North blew smoke toward the ceiling, "But she's only twenty-five. She should be tough enough to fight this thing."

The doctor examined her chart that hung on the footboard, "Her parents told us that she suffered a trauma this summer. Severe dehydration that she nearly died from?"

"That's right."

"It may have weakened her enough to be susceptible. It really is hard to tell why some people get sicker than others." He replaced the chart and put his hands in his lab coat pockets.

"So, how long until she's up and about?" North tried to sound upbeat; he was pretty sure he'd failed.

"I'm going to be honest with you," the doctor looked down. "If her fever doesn't drop within the next twenty-four hours, I'm not certain she'll survive."

"But, she still has a chance, right?" there was an edge in North's voice.

"Well, yes, there is…"

North cut the doctor off mid-sentence, "Than you better do everything you can. My name's North. You can leave a message for me with the Sheriff's Office in Howell. I want to know the minute anything changes with her condition." He turned toward the door, then turned back to face the doctor notepad in hand, "What's your name?"

"Dobson, Dr. Norman Dobson."

"And your phone number?"

"Normandy 2-3428."

North flipped the notepad closed and left the hospital. He spent the drive back to Hell thinking about the events of the past seven days. Three women had been killed, one traumatized, two missing cars, and one murderer in the morgue. Even with everything that had gone on, North honestly did not give a fuck. He checked his watch, eleven on a Sunday morning. Other than a church, there was no place open; at least no place he wanted to go, especially with his head wrapped like Boris Karloff in the Mummy.

He pulled the pickup into the drive of the cottage and sat in it instead of going inside. Other than the pain emanating from the back of his head, North was numb. Nothing mattered, not his job back in LaSalle Harbor, not the upcoming criminal case against him, not the pain in his skull. Nothing. The only thing that mattered was a petite blonde in a hospital bed seventeen miles away. There was no enemy he was afraid of, but how can you fight something you cannot see?

North was alone. Not just sitting in a pickup in a deserted township next to an empty cottage. But genuinely alone. Everyone he had ever truly cared about was gone. His mother, friends who had died in the war, and now the possibility of Sylvia dying. It was all too much.

His shoulders began to shake, and lowering his head onto the back of his hands that rested on the steering wheel, he cried. Tears ran down his face and saturated the cuffs of the grey suit jacket. Each tear darkened the fabric a little more until the cuffs appeared more black than grey.

Finally, he snuffed the tears back up his nose and walked inside. The cottage was just as he had left it; blood and brains on the floor and the wall and furniture in disarray. He changed his clothes, grabbed a bucket and a rag, and began to clean. At some point, he laid down in the bedroom and fell asleep to Sylvia's scent on the pillow.

He awoke in the dark. The cottage was cold. His bladder was full, and Gatto was howling to be let in. "Hey, bub. Guess you're probably hungry," North said as he bent down and scratched the cat's ears. He dropped some cat food onto a plate; Gatto grabbed for it before the plate ever made it to the floor. The stove finally lit, the room began to warm.

North took a sip of bourbon and watched the cat chase the plate across the room.

Having watched the cat eat reminded North that he had not eaten anything in a day and a half. He poured a bowl of Wheaties and washed them down with more Old Quaker. When he finally checked his watch, he was surprised to see that it was only half-past ten. It was going to be a long night.

Chapter 25

Monday morning found Barry Tiffin cautiously arriving at the office. He now felt the presence of something he never had previously, enemies. Every car he passed, every pedestrian he saw was, potentially, someone sent to kill him.

He parked the Ford Mainline the detective squad shared in the lot behind the building. He took the elevator to the second floor. The moment the doors opened, he saw two State Police troopers talking with the Chief.

"Barry!" Chief Cummings shouted, "you need to hear this."

"What's up, Chief?" Tiffin said as he lit a cigarette.

One of the troopers spoke up, "Those men we took into custody Saturday night at your house have criminal records that include felony assault and battery on a peace officer, battery causing great bodily harm, receiving stolen weapons, kidnapping, and grand theft."

"Bad hombres," Tiffin took a drag on his smoke, "who were they working for?"

"This is where it gets interesting," Cummings jumped in.

The trooper continued, "Both of them had spent time in the state pen, and both of them received early release at the request of the Attorney General's office."

Tiffin was visibly shaken, "Do you know who in the AG's office signed off on that?"

"Yes, one Charles Coosard by name."

"Coosard," Tiffin thought for a moment as he rolled the name around in his head. "Charles Coosard! He's the one that got Brick brought up on charges."

Cummings pulled the pipe from between his teeth, "As Brick would say, there's no such thing as a coincidence." He looked at the troopers, "Does the FBI have this information?"

"They do. We're keeping them updated on everything we find."

"There's no telling how far the rot has spread," the chief mused.

With a promise to keep each other updated, the troopers left. Cummings spoke in a paternal tone, "Did Kaye and the kids get to her brothers okay?"

"Yes. But I don't need to tell you how reluctant she was to go." Tiffin looked around the squad room, "Where's Uher?"

Cummings rolled his wrist over and looked at his watch, "Half-past eight. He should have been here half an hour ago. When's the last time you heard from him?"

"Yesterday evening when we left."

"Do you know where he's staying?

"With his wife in Ludington, he's staying at his house." Tiffin felt a rush of adrenaline mixed with anxiety; it did not make a good cocktail.

"Grab a couple of uniformed officers and get over to his house." Cummings looked at Tiffin with concern, "And Barry, be careful."

"Thanks, Chief," Tiffin called the Sergeant's desk and arranged for two officers to rendezvous with him at the Uher residence on Hoyt Street. Tiffin arrived before the radio car. He waited down the block for the officers to show up.

The Uher residence was one of the few one-story bungalows on the block. One officer and Tiffin climbed onto the front porch while the other officer walked around back. Tiffin looked through the window but couldn't make anything out. The front door was locked. Just as they stepped off the porch, the second officer called out, "Detective! I've got an unlocked door back here."

Tiffin ran around the back of the house as the officer stepped away from the door, "I didn't go in. I just tried the knob to see if it was open."

"Okay, let's see what we've got," Tiffin drew his revolver from the holster on his waist. The two officers followed suit. He turned the knob and pushed the door; it opened onto a small landing. Three steps led up into the kitchen, a flight of steps led down into the basement. "Police!" Tiffin shouted. There was no response.

Tiffin used his head to point to one of the officers, "Stay here. No one comes in, no one goes out." The officer nodded his understanding.

The other officer followed the detective into the kitchen. Tiffin had begun to walked past the table when he lifted his hand, stopping the officer. He looked at a piece of paper on the table. Written in block letters were the words, 'You're a dead man!' The pair walked through the kitchen into the dining room and then the living room. One of the two bedrooms showed signs of having been slept in, and there was a damp towel in the bathroom.

"Well, he was here," the officer observed.

Walking back through the kitchen, Tiffin nodded toward the basement, "Let's take a look downstairs."

The wooden stairs creaked under their weight as they entered the low-ceilinged space. A wringer washer stood near a utility sink to their right. An oversized furnace occupied most of the basement center, its asbestos-wrapped ducts reaching out to each of the rooms upstairs. There was a coal room near the heater and various boxes, suitcases, and other cast-off items on the space's far side. But no Dan Uher.

Outside, they closed the door and checked out the garage on the back of the lot. The only entrance was the double door on the front, which was securely locked. Tiffin walked around the side and used his hand to brush away dirt to peer in. He couldn't make out much but saw neither a car nor Uher.

One of the officers looked at Tiffin, "What's next?"

"Let's go two houses down on either side and across the street. Ask everyone who answers if they know the Uhers and if anyone has seen anything suspicious. We'll meet back here." The three were back together within five minutes. "You come up with anything?" Tiffin asked. Both officers indicated they had not. "Then I thank you for your time. You're free to go."

"Thank you, sir," one of the officers said as they walked back to their car.

"Okay, Dan. Where the hell are you," Tiffin mumbled toward the house. He was back at the Safety Building within five minutes. As he was climbing the terrazzo stairs to the squad room as Uher was heading down.

"I wouldn't go up there!" Uher bemoaned, "Cummings is pissed off!"

"You think the chief is pissed?!" Tiffin spat back.

"What did I do?"

"When you didn't show up on time, we figured something happened to you. Two unis and I just canvassed your neighborhood and searched your house looking for you."

"I stopped at the Fifth Wheel and got some breakfast. No big deal."

"No big deal! What about the note on your table that says you're a dead man?"

"Millie left that for me. Guess she wanted me to know how mad she is."

Tiffin gave Uher a once over, "So, where are you going?"

"Cummings told me to get out of his sight, so I thought I'd better leave."

In a voice that was almost a growl, Tiffin threatened, "Just get your ass back to your desk and get to work!"

Uher pulled himself up to his full height, "You're not my superior."

"No, I'm your fucking nanny, and your work is a reflection on me. Now get back up these stairs!"

"Geez. Everyone is on the rag today."

Tiffin shook his head as he followed Uher up the stairs, "And you probably wonder why your wife left you."

Chapter 26

North made a pot of coffee and fried the pork chops and potatoes that he had planned on feeding Sylvia. For a moment, he thought about a shot of bourbon but reconsidered. Nelson was dead, but he still needed to file the paperwork. And there were still two cars missing. After downing the pot of coffee, shaving, and getting dressed, he was on his way back to Howell.

"Any calls for me?" he shouted as he walked into the Sheriff's Office.

Joyce looked up, "My God, Brick. Tom said you got roughed up, but I wasn't expecting this! You okay?"

"Never better, doll," North lied. "Any calls for me?"

"None. You expecting a call from the hospital about," Joyce paused as she recalled the name, "Sylvia?"

He nodded, "That's right."

"Did you see her yesterday?" the concern in the receptionist's voice was genuine.

"I was there for a while. She wasn't awake."

"Did the doctors tell you anything about what's going on?"

North pulled out a cigarette and lit it, "Something called meningitis."

"I've heard of that. Is she going to be okay?"

"I don't know, Joyce. I don't know. All I can gather is that she's really sick."

"I'll keep her in my thoughts. By the way, Wilma's funeral is at ten this morning. If you're going, can I catch a ride with you? The Sheriff is going right from his house."

For just a moment, North toyed with saying no, "Yeah, I'm going. Is it here in town?"

"It's at St. John's on Hacker Road. I'll be the navigator if you'd like."

"Sure, doll. That'll be great. I'm going to finish up my report on Nelson. Let me know when it's time to go." North walked over to the coffee urn and poured a cup before settling at the desk he was using. Rolling a form into the Underwood typewriter's carriage, he began to fill in the blanks. North considered himself the king of three-finger typing, index fingers for the letters, and his right thumb for the space bar. The slow tap-tap-tap was interrupted by the occasional zip of the carriage return lever. The mountain of cigarette butts in the ashtray gave evidence to the intensity of his work.

Joyce looked over North's shoulder as he typed, "You're actually pretty good considering that seven of your fingers are just along for the ride."

North chuckled, "Is it time to go?" as he turned and paid attention to Joyce's black suit and black hat with a small black veil that draped in front of her eyes.

"You approve?" she said as she gave a little twirl.

"I didn't know you had legs," he smirked as he put the form he had been working on into a folder which he placed into a desk drawer.

"That's because I'm always sitting at my desk."

St. John's reminded Brick enough of St. Julian's back in LaSalle Harbor that he wondered if all Catholic churches were built from the same set of plans. The priest, clothed in black, followed a young boy swinging a brass ball on the end of a chain. Smoke billowed from the ball. The priest stopped at the casket of Wilma Deweiss and greeted Dennis, their daughter, and other family members.

"*In Nomine Patris et Filii et Spiritus Sancti,*" the priest intoned.

Those gathered made the sign of the cross over themselves as they said, "*Amen.*"

The priest continued, "*Requiem aeternam dona eis...*" North let his mind wander as the priest intoned his incantations. He watched as Robert Eberhart from the mortuary guided the pallbearers as they wheeled the casket down the aisle. The family followed and took their position in the front pew. North focused on Deweiss, who seemed old, small, and frail, in stark contrast to the man he had worked with just days before.

As the Mass continued, North began to feel the heaviness of the events that had happened the past few days: Dennis's display of grief as he voiced his wife's death. Sylvia's illness and the uncertainty of what was happening to her. The young punk who had tried to kill him. He thought about what Dennis must be feeling and recognized that grief overtook and controlled a person; it wasn't a feeling. The weight of grief he realized he carried suddenly overtook him, and North quietly wept. A few days ago, he had wondered if he could ever feel for someone like Deweiss felt for his wife. At that moment, he knew that he could because that was how he thought about Sylvia. The fact that he never told her weighed on him. The sadness closed his ears. Except for the hand that wove its way into his fingers, he was alone.

"You crying for Wilma or Sylvia?" Joyce whispered.

He tried to say Sylvia, but the word wouldn't come.

After Mass, North and Joyce sat in the pickup. She leaned over and put her head on his shoulder, "I wish someone cared for me the way you care for her." She straightened up and gently kissed him on the cheek. "I hope she gets better."

"Thanks, I hope so too." North lit a cigarette, started the truck, and turned back to the office.

They had just entered the office when one of the young deputies approached. "Uh, Deputy North?" he spent a moment staring at North's bandaged head, "We just got a call from a farmer outside of Pinckney. Says he's got a couple of cars down by a ravine that don't belong there."

North pulled the notepad from his pocket, "What kind of cars?"

"Says ones a nearly new yellow Chevy with a white top."

North cut him off, "And the other is a blue Mercury with a grey fender."

"How did you know that?"

"You'd know it too if you'd keep your eye on the bulletins on the board." North sighed, "You just going to stand there, or are you going to get us a car to drive to this farm?"

The twenty-minute drive was completed pretty much in silence. North smoked and watched the farmland go by. The young deputy drove quietly, afraid to ask North any questions. The silence was okay as far as Brick was concerned.

The Livingston County Sheriff's vehicle pulled into the drive of an old white farmhouse. They were just exiting the car when the farmer stepped out onto the porch, "Get back in the car. I'll show you what I found." He climbed into the back seat.

"Go back out to the main road and turn west. The cars are at the edge of my property line. A half-mile down the lane, the farmer had them turn onto a dirt two-track. They followed it less than a hundred feet when he had them stop. "Just down here," he directed with his forehead.

North and the deputy exited the car and walked down the embankment. The two vehicles faced uphill and nose out. "Yep, these look like what we're looking for." They slid their way down the ravine where North tried the driver's door of the Chevy. It opened as he pushed the button. On the floorboard was a brown leather purse. He dug inside and pulled out the billfold. The Ohio operator's permit was for a Helen Krawczyk. In the change purse was a simple yellow wedding band. North looked in the middle of the band. The initials BK and SD were engraved, along with 3-14-49.

"Anything in the other car?" North called to the deputy.

"There's a wallet in the glove box."

"Any ID?"

"Yeah, Michigan driver's license and a University ID card."

"Are there names on either of those?" North's frustration grew.

The deputy called back, "Monica Baker?"

"Is there a question there, deputy?"

"Ah, no, sir."

"Grab the wallet," he called back to the deputy. North walked back up the ravine to the farmer, "You okay if we use your phone? We'll arrange to get these cars out of here."

"Stolen, are they?" the farmer asked.

"Not exactly. Both belong to dead women."

The farmer turned ashen, "They weren't killed here, were they?"

"No, sir. They were killed elsewhere. Just their cars were dumped here."

The farmer breathed deeply, "Well, thank God for that." He paused for a moment and shook his head, "I don't mean that it's good that they're dead."

North gave a half-smile, "Yeah, you mean what I know."

They arranged to have the cars towed back to the office and thanked the farmer for his time. "I'm guessing there ain't no reward or nothing," he inquired.

North shook his head, "Afraid not. Come on, deputy. Let's get going."

Back in Howell, North called his counterpart in the Sheriff's Office in Washtenaw County. "Art Chadwick."

"Chadwick, North here. We've got Monica Baker's killer and her car."

Chadwick's voice jumped up, "You've caught the sonofabitch?"

The lid to North's Zippo clicked shut, "Not exactly."

"What does that mean?" Chadwick laughed.

North took a satisfying drag on the Pall Mall, "It means that he won't be hurting anyone else."

"He's dead?"

"Unfortunately, he didn't leave me a choice," North touched the bandages on the back of his head.

Chadwick leaned forward in his seat, "Did he try to shoot you?"

"Nothing so delicate. He hit me in the head with an ax."

"Holy shit. Guess it's good you're hard-headed!"

"Do me a favor, will you," North asked as he drew in another lungfull of smoke.

"What's that?"

"When you let Withers know about Monica's killer being caught, let him know that we haven't located his engagement ring. When it's found, we'll make sure he gets it."

"Will do. Is Monica's car drivable?"

"It's a bit beat up from being rolled into a ravine, but I imagine it should run fine."

"Where's it located?"

"It'll be here at the Livingston County Sheriff's Office."

"Hey, Brick," Chadwick boomed, "it's been good working with you. You going to stay on working with Drake?"

"No, Art. I think I'm going to finish my reports and hand in my badge."

North pressed the switchhook, disconnecting his call with Chadwick. When he released it, the phone on Joyce' switchboard buzzed, "What can I do for you, Brick?"

"Get me Doug Milner down with the Toledo PD."

"Okay. I'm on it."

North crushed the cigarette out, "Thanks, doll." He began to rhythmically tap more entries into his report. Ten minutes passed before the phone rang, "Hold for Detective Milner." There were a couple of clicks before the line was connected.

"North?" Milner queried.

"Thought you'd want to know that we found that fifty-five Chevy you've been looking for."

"That's good news. What kind of shape is it in?"

"Well, it was found in the bottom of a ravine. So, let's leave it at driveable."

"That'll teach the dealership to be careful about who they let take a car on a test drive," Milner chuckled.

North paused as he flipped through his notepad, "One more thing."

"Yeah, what's that?"

"There was a purse in the car. The operator's permit says that it was owned by a Helen Krawczyk." North spelled the name for Milner, pronouncing it 'craw-zik.'

"Craw-check," Milner corrected. "The name is pronounced craw-check."

"You know who this is?" North asked.

"Neighbors noticed a foul odor coming from the Krawczyk house. When they checked it out, they found Mr. Basil Krawczyk stabbed to death in the dining room. The coroner figured he'd been dead four or five days."

"Was there a child? Our coroner said she'd had given birth at least once."

"From what we can gather from their extended family, they had a daughter who died last spring at the age of five. It looks like Helen blamed Basil for the child's death."

"I've seen people murder for less," North pulled a cigarette out of the package and held it between his lips. "Any idea why she blamed him?"

"Guess he didn't believe in doctors or something. Wouldn't let her take the girl to see one when the girl got sick."

"So, Basil not letting Helen take the child to the doctor basically killed the child. Helen kills him, and a gas-pump jockey named Jimmy Nelson kills Helen." There was a pause on the line, "Milner, you still with me?"

"Dammit! I should have figured this out," he finally said.

"How's that?" North lit his cigarette.

"Krawczyk is Polish for Tailor. Helen Krawczyk became Helen Tailor when she stole that car. It was right before my eyes, and I didn't see it."

"Don't beat yourself up, pal. Looks like you've closed two cases," North took a drag in the Pall Mall. "I'll mail you a copy of my report."

"Thanks, North." Milner disconnected the call.

North replaced the receiver and walked up to the reception desk, "Joyce, I'm going to go grab some lunch."

"People are going to talk, what with you wearing that turban and all," she teased.

"Let 'em," he smiled as he turned toward the door. "Be back in forty-five minutes or so." He had almost made it to the door when Joyce called after him. He turned, "What's up?"

"Phone call for you."

He took the call at the reception desk. "Richard North," he answered. "Yes, I am," there was a long pause. "What? When?"

Joyce stood up so that Brick could sit.

Chapter 27

A quarter past nine on Tuesday morning found Cummings, Tiffin, and Uher standing outside the Douglas County Sheriff's Office. At six, the FBI had called the chief at home to let him know they would be conducting a multipronged operation. Several uniformed LaSalle Police officers stood at the ready alongside the chief and two detectives, should they be needed. There were also reporters sent by their editors after Cummings called with an ambiguous message about big news.

At nine-thirty, shutters began to click as FBI agents led Sheriff Red Wilson out. Wilson, hands cuffed behind his back, tried to hide his face from both the cameras and the reporter's questions. Three deputies were also lead out in cuffs.

In a well-timed operation, other agents arrested the Douglas County District Attorney and several City Councilmen. While that was happening in LaSalle Harbor, agents entered the Attorney General's office in Lansing and took Charles Coosard into custody.

By midday, news had spread about the incredible level of corruption taking place not just in Douglas County but throughout Michigan. Oftermatt had bribed or blackmailed many who wielded influence.

Back at the Safety Building, the chief called Tiffin into his office, "First," he began, "I want to thank you for the excellent work you did."

"Thank you, Chief."

"The evidence you found broke this thing wide open. If Wilson's boys had gotten those ledgers and photos, we'd have never known what he was up to."

Tiffin shook his head, "There'll be more dirty politicians to take the place of those who were picked up today."

"No doubt," Cummings started packing his pipe. "But we've set corruption on its ear. At least for a while."

"You said, first. What else do you have for me?"

"Take Uher. Find Oftermatt's kid. It's time for some justice."

By noon Bobby Oftermatt was screaming to be released from his holding cell. "Shut up, kid," Lou called down the cell block, "I'm trying to finish today's crossword."

Within days, Cummings learned from the Attorney General that the Grand Jury that had recommended North be indicted had members who were recipients of gifts from Oftermatt. "You've got to see that North was set up," the chief argued. "This isn't justice!" He heard the rustle of paper.

"Exactly what evidence was there against your Detective North?" the AG asked as he flipped through the file.

"There was no evidence. There was only the word of a rapist."

"Witnesses?"

"Just another detective who was helping escort the prisoner to the cells." Cummings held the receiver against his shoulder as he packed his pipe.

The AG paused while he reviewed the file, "In looking through the file, I don't see where there's enough evidence to get a conviction. I'm at a loss over why this case was ever taken up."

Cummings coaxed flame into the tobacco in his pipe, "Maybe this wasn't about a conviction. Maybe this was about ruining North's career."

"For argument's sake," the AG offered, "why would anyone want to ruin his career?"

"Evil can only thrive in the absence of honest men."

Chapter 28

North had repacked Sylvia's suitcase and cosmetic bag and taken them to Ann Arbor. There he had them put on a train for her parents to pick up at the Michigan Central Station in Detroit. Before closing the suitcase, he enclosed a letter addressed to them.

Dear Mr. & Mrs. Kingston,

I would like to express my deepest condolences on the death of your daughter. Sylvia was so much more than a friend. I had recently come to realize that I wanted to spend the rest of my life with her. At this time, I should be asking you for her hand and not writing a letter to offer my sympathy.

You raised a loving, caring, and kindhearted woman. She had many friends and was deeply respected in her job with the police department. I will forever miss her.

Sincerely,
Richard North

Back at North's End, Brick pulled the holster off his shoulders and hung it over the back of one of the kitchen chairs. He grabbed a jelly jar and the bottle of Old Quaker and fell back onto the sofa. He had never felt so lost or so tired in his life.

A knock on the door woke him from a vivid dream of Sylvia laughing over a dish of tiramisu. North pulled the Colt free from its leather binding and looked through one of the front door windows. A young man stood anxiously outside. North pulled the door open and pointed the .38 at the youth. "What do you want?"

"Telegram for Rick North," the kid managed to stutter.

"Sorry, kid," North lowered the gun. Reaching into his pocket North grabbed a dollar bill that he handed the youth in exchange for the yellow envelope. Gatto forced his way past the Western Union carrier and North.

"Thanks, Mister!"

North sat back on the sofa; Gatto jumped up next to him. He unfolded the note and read,

> Case against you dismissed. Look forward to your return.
> Chief Cummings.

He balled up the telegram and tossed it across the room. Gatto kneaded the sofa for a moment before falling against North's leg. North scratched the cat's ears before he leaned back and closed his eyes. Perhaps, the thought, he could get back to that dream.

A sneak preview of the next Brick North Mystery

AUGUSTINE MEIJER

Sand Rabbit
Murders
A Brick North Mystery

Chapter 1

North handed the forty-five hundred dollar check to the agent. It was the biggest check he had ever written. He had also just broken the promise he'd made to himself that he would never buy a house. But, here he was, being handed the keys to a two-bedroom bungalow on the lakefront.

After his discharge from the army, North had spent years living in boarding houses. After tiring of boarding houses, he had lived in the Swanson Hotel for two years, which offered only slightly more privacy. Months of living in his parent's cottage in Hell changed his mind about homeownership. Having a private bathroom and a kitchen was better than he'd imagined.

Vine Street was below the bluff that overlooked Lake Michigan. The houses were predominately occupied by factory and shop workers. Like all the others, his place was built on a shallow foundation situated upon the white sands for which Lake Michigan was famous. Two blocks from the beach, his property backed up to the tracks; freight and passenger trains rumbled past throughout the day and night.

With some used furniture in place, North set up residence. The cat that had adopted him while in Hell made himself at home. Having investigated every room and closet, Gatto called dibs on the wing chair in the living room. From there, he could sun himself and keep an eye on the comings and goings through the neighborhood. He seemed most interested in the children who made their way to the stairs that led up the bluff and their school.

A few blocks from North's new home was the Silver Beach Amusement Park, closed now for the winter. The most imposing feature of the area was the empty factory that had been the Cooper Wells Hosiery Company. The three- and four-story Cooper Wells buildings had been vacant since fifty-two when the factory closed. Pigeons and vagrants occupied spaces where once knitting machines churned out socks and stockings.

Deep in the original building's basement was a secret that at least one person hoped would remain buried.

Made in the USA
Coppell, TX
13 May 2023